Death in Hades Wells

MB Morrigan

RAVEN ROAD
BOOKS

©2024 MB Morrigan

This is entirely a work of fiction. Any resemblance to actual persons, living or dead, places or events is coincidental.

Dedicated to my family, for all the support, love and laughter. And to the cats, always loving and always there.

1

It was early morning. The sun was slowly rising over the stark, barren mountains, bathing the desert in a soft orange glow. The parched land was empty of humanity, the town was clustered down in the valley, close to the water of the Colorado River as it snaked its way through the arid country. The plants, cactus, palo verde and mesquite, all seemed to glow in the soft dawn light. The air was dry, giving the landscape sharp outlines. The ground was beginning to warm up, and there was a hint of the scorching heat that would arrive later in the day.

A solitary vehicle was slowly winding its way across the desert floor, away from the last traces of civilization, following a dry streambed up towards the red and black mountains. The dust from the vehicle rose like a cloud and gently dispersed in the morning wind. The arroyo—locals called it a wash—served as something of a highway for people moving to and from the mountains. Hikers, hunters, gold prospectors and the occasional archaeologist all drove up the wash, chancing disaster in the form of a flash flood every time they did. Doctor Duncan Keogh, adjunct professor of archaeology, slowed the car down, prolonging his arrival at work just a little longer.

As he reached for his coffee, he flipped the radio on. "Good morning," the DJ chimed. "It's going to be a lovely day here. Clear skies are expected with a high around 115, wind from the south 15 to 25 miles an hour, low overnight 85, it's currently a brisk 92 out there. Looks like 2003 is shaping up to be a hot one, folks! Here's a good one for you, something from Van Halen's first album."

Duncan looked moodily at the radio, running a hand through his shaggy dark hair. He glanced in the rearview mirror, his eyes had dark circles under them, his face red with sunburn. *Only in Hell and Hades Wells is 115 considered a lovely day.* The bitter thought formed for the hundredth time.

He finally understood why being sent to head the university's major archaeological project in the valley was not an honor, just the opposite in fact. He finally understood why his colleagues called it getting sent to hell for the summer. And more than anything else he finally understood why you never, ever told Professor Jeremy Martin, Chair of the Department of Archaeology at John Wesley Powell University, that he didn't know what he was talking about. No matter if you were the second youngest Ph.D. ever awarded by the department, no, even then you had to watch your step, because the good professor had a temper and a very good idea of the concept and execution of Hammurabian justice.

Duncan turned out of the wash and up onto the road that led to the site. He was dreading his arrival, every morning since the project began, getting to work was miserable. Complaints and sarcasm served up daily with his morning coffee.

The students, being students, had to live on site under the supervision of Marlee Kennet, a TA at the department. None of them, especially Marlee, were happy that he got to return to a house every night while they lived in tents with sand, bugs and no air conditioning. It was the only real nod to his position as head of the project. And they hated him for it, especially since he was closer to their age than most project heads, so he was considered one of them, not the boss. As he pulled up to the site he hit a bump, the same bump he hit every morning, and spilled coffee over his bare legs.

The students were already up and about, moving around the campsite. He could smell coffee and bacon in the morning air. He parked his car next to the lab trailer and got out, stretching his back, glad that the coffee had spilled onto bare skin and not fabric.

"Morning, Duncan," Marlee said, walking up to him and handing him a cup of coffee. She looked down at his legs with a smirk.

"Morning, anything interesting happening?" It was part of the morning ritual, as was her answer of "the usual."

"The usual." She shrugged. "Unless you consider the burial."

"The what?!" His head snapped up and he looked at her with a frown. "What did you say?"

"Burial, found him just after you left last night, would have called but you know the cell reception out here is pretty bad." She was taunting him, he knew it, she knew it. "Some of us didn't even go to sleep. I made them stop for breakfast," she said as they walked through the project site. "Only, I thought the locals didn't bury their dead. I thought they cremated."

Duncan took a sip of his coffee. "You're right, cremation was common, in fact when the army got here, they passed a law that someone had to be dead for a day or two prior to cremation. They claimed some people were cremated early."

"Do you think it could be an earlier culture then? The one that made those chert axes?"

"Could be," Duncan said with a grin. "It could also be our ticket out of Hell."

She grinned back. "I hadn't thought of that, I should have come and got you last night. Oh, well, next time, right? Here we are."

Duncan didn't need to be told, the sweet-sick smell of death had been getting stronger as they got closer to the dig area. It now hung over him like a cloud, filling his lungs, making him gag. He looked down into the trench at the carefully excavated body, still half held in the grip of the earth. Something struck him as odd. He hopped down next to the partially mummified body. "Smells nice," he said to Marlee.

"Yeah, can you imagine working in a tomb in Egypt? Must stink to high heaven." She crouched down at the edge of the trench. "We thought it was a ritual killing of some kind, look at his neck."

Duncan took a deep breath and squatted down beside the mummy. He took a long look at the partially de-fleshed throat, the stone tool sticking out of the trachea at an angle. He pulled his pocketknife out and poked at it very gently trying to get a better look at it. Obsidian, biface, large and... "Shit," he said aloud. "It *is* going to be one of those days."

"What is it?" Marlee said as he pulled himself out of the trench.

"Get everyone out of here, have them work on that factory site down on the ridge. I'll be back."

"What is it?" she repeated. "Where are you going?"

"Driving back to town," he said with a sigh. "To get the police."

2

The few remaining morning commuters were frantically trying to get through town. The heat of the day was beginning to become palpable, warming the pavement, causing mirage to appear on the highway running through the center of town. Captain Ignacio "Nate" Mondragon, deputy chief of police, was fighting the traffic with everyone else, the temptation to turn on lights and sirens to force his way through a work zone starting to become an obsession.

It was going to be one of those days, he could feel it in his bones with a certainty born of long experience. Of course, most days during the summer in Hades Wells could be classed as one of those days, he thought with a snort. If it wasn't a tourist dying from overexposure, it was a tourist dying in a jet-ski accident, or a tourist buying bad drugs from the people who offered such commodities up and down the river. Or someone driving too fast, or someone shooting someone because they were hot and cranky. He sighed and finished his second cup of coffee, finally pulling up behind the station.

Some days, he questioned his choice to take a job in the small town, but at the end of the day, he never regretted the decision. Hades Wells was small—5000 people in the "greater metro" area, but because of its unique location between several larger vacation areas and across the Colorado from Nevada, there was more for his department to do than a town three times the size elsewhere. In fact, he had a fairly large police force, all things considered. They had to cover not only the "metro" area, but thousands of acres that were part of the larger area around the town that he was expected to keep reasonably crime free.

He had a feeling this would be a six cup of coffee day—he could always tell. The day before had been filled with paperwork, a "sit down" with an officer who had several complaints about his behavior and more paperwork. Then as he had settled in for the night, he had been pulled from his few precious hours' sleep by an accident investigation downtown, a drunk had plowed into a pedestrian at somewhat more than one hundred miles an hour. The motorist fled the scene—and the pedestrian? There had hardly been enough left of him to scrape up and put in a body bag.

"Morning, Sal," he said to his secretary, Sally Blackburn, as he walked into his office.

"Good morning, Nate, you look like hell," she said.

"Thanks. I feel like hell. Please tell me the coffee is ready?"

"Not only ready, but I poured you a cup a few minutes ago so it would be the proper degree of tepid when you arrived."

He grinned at her. "Bless you, remind me to give you a raise, okay?"

"Already wrote it on the next check."

"Good, saves me the trouble. And, you know, I'm pretty sure tepid is actually a temperature," he said, picking up the cup of coffee beside the pot and taking a sip. As promised it was cool enough to drink.

"Tepid is a temperature? You have been spending too much time with Dizzy again," she said.

"My dear Sal, any time with Diz can be too much time."

"Sure, it is, I rest my case."

He laughed and walked into his office. Paperwork covered nearly every horizontal surface. He sighed as he looked at the various piles of files and reports he needed to get through. Somehow being deputy chief brought on more headaches than being a beat cop, and most of those headaches involved paperwork. It was never ending.

Sometime later the office intercom beeped, demanding his attention, pulling him from the report of, improbably enough, an accident involving a truck carrying chicken and another carrying rice. "What?" Nate snapped.

"Sorry to bother you, sir, but there is someone here who wants to report a body," Sal said.

"And? Tell him to talk to whoever is on duty," he said.

"They, uh, they sent him back to you, sir."

"All right, I'll be right out." He should have known from her tone, he should have known from her repeated use of "sir." He picked up his coffee, cup number six, and walked out of the office.

A tall man with longish brown hair stood at Sal's desk. From the smile on her face, Nate could tell she thought he was attractive, probably something about his eyes. Sal had a thing for eyes. Nate chuckled silently. The man was dressed in typical tourist desert wear: shorts, short-sleeved shirt, boots and no hat. He showed all the signs that he hadn't learned the lesson of staying covered in the midday sun. He was sunburned on his face, arms and legs.

"I'm Captain Mondragon," Nate said, holding out his hand. "What can I do for you?"

"I'm Dr. Duncan Keogh," the other said, shaking the extended hand. "I'm in charge of the JW Powell University project east of town."

"Yes?"

"Well, we found a burial and I thought I should report it."

Nate looked at him in disbelief. "You found a burial?" Keogh nodded. "And for some reason you need to report it to the police? Is that some new archaeologist rule? You have to report burials to the police? God, I'm glad I'm not a cop in Egypt."

"Oh, ha ha," Keogh said. "I wouldn't be here if I thought it was prehistoric, or even historic. I'm pretty sure it's recent, like within the last five years, maybe."

"Really? Oh, well in that case, let's discuss it in my office." Nate turned to Sal. "You want to give Diz a call and have her come down?"

"No," she said, looking at him. "You call."

"Come on, Sal, call."

"No. I'll roll a uniform out there, but I won't call Dizzy."

"Fine, I'll call, but there goes that raise," he said, stalking into his office.

"I'd trade the raise for calling her with something like this any day. And the whole raise is worth the look on your face…uh, sir," she said, standing and pulling the door closed behind them.

"Let me make this call," Nate said to Keogh as he sat back behind his desk. He turned the speaker phone on and hit speed dial.

"What do you want?" she answered on the third ring.

"What are you doing?" he said, looking at the phone as if he were talking to her in person.

"Getting coffee and heading by your office before I do that survey. Figured you might be dead from lack of caffeine."

"Great, thanks. I have the head of the JW Powell University project here, he says he found a burial," he said, smiling, knowing what was coming.

"That's what archaeologists are supposed to do, isn't it. You tell him that?"

"I tried, Diz, but he said it's recent." He looked up at Keogh, the other man was frowning.

"A perfect excuse to avoid that survey again. I'll be there in ten minutes. Does the archaeologist want coffee?"

Nate raised his eyebrows enquiringly at Keogh. "Uh, yeah, sure," he said to Nate. "A low-fat, sugar-free vanilla latte would be great."

"He wants a what?"

"You heard him, Diz, just get it and come on, okay?"

"Can't Sal order that? How will I ever live down ordering something like that? I'll have to change espresso stands, they'll all laugh at me," she said.

"Order the damn coffee and get down here," Nate said a bit sharper than he intended.

"Someone is owly this morning. Fine. I'll be right there." The connection broke with a snap.

"She's a character," Nate said, looking up at Keogh.

"Who is she?"

"Dizzy Donovan, our local expert, she runs the Baxter Institute and helps identify bits before we send them off to the medical examiner."

"Your local expert, who runs an institute, is named Dizzy?" Keogh said, disbelief apparent in his voice.

"Don't worry, it's not like dizzy blonde, no, it's just that when you're around her—well, after a while your head starts to spin," Nate laughed. "Now, you want to tell me why you think this is a recent burial?"

"State of the body for one thing, decomposition and the beginnings of mummification, but not well underway. He had a point shoved in his neck that, if I'm not mistaken, not only shouldn't be in this valley, but should not exist on this continent and..." Keogh paused for effect.

"You know, Dr. Keogh, you are being very dramatic for this early in the morning," Nate said sourly.

"I've been up since five."

"Lovely, I suppose you run, too? Can I hear what the big 'and' was for?"

"He's wearing a wristwatch."

"What?"

"Seiko, I think, I didn't think it was a good idea to pull his arm out and take a really good look until I came in and talked to the police."

"Thanks," Nate said, looking at him. "This will be so much fun, nothing Diz likes more than a decomposing body in the morning. She claims it goes great with coffee."

"This Dizzy of yours sounds like quite the sage."

"I am not a Dizzy of anybody," a female voice said from the door. "So, don't get any ideas about that. Morning, Nate, you look like hell."

"People keep telling me that. I think it has something to do with no sleep and early morning body scraping." Nate looked up and smiled at Dizzy. She was dressed in her usual work clothes, jeans, a long-sleeved shirt and sandals. Silver earrings dangled from her ears.

She handed him a large paper cup of coffee. "There's a happy morning thought." She turned around and looked up at Keogh. "Here is your, well, I can't really call it coffee, can I? They laughed at me. Laughed."

"What do you drink?" Keogh said, looking down at her.

"Americano, six shots, splash of soymilk, one sugar. I'm Dizzy Donovan, you?"

"Dr. Duncan Keogh," he said, holding out his hand.

"Ah, the prodigy, second-youngest Ph.D. at Powell U, right?" She grinned at Keogh. "How did you manage to get sent here to hell for the summer if you're the *wunderkind*? Mouth off to Martin?"

Keogh was looking at her with shock on his face. "How did you know?"

"I have my sources," she said. "News like that filters out pretty fast, you know. I heard you told him, flat out, that he was wrong. Are you even a tiny bit surprised you ended up here, Dr. Keogh?"

"I have to maintain integrity," Keogh said defensively.

"Diz?" Nate said, stepping in before he had a bloodbath in his office. "Let's not tease the archaeologist, okay?"

"Not teasing," she said. "Why am I here again?"

"Dr. Keogh found a burial. He came in to report it."

"Oh, right, and you already told him that's in the job description, right? Or is that some new archaeologist rule? You have to report all that stuff to the cops?"

"Everyone is a comedian this morning, great," Keogh said, looking from one to the other. "Heat, students, only recently dead bodies and comedy. This is such a lovely day already."

"Did I miss something?" Dizzy said.

"I said pretty much the same thing when he came in." Nate glanced at the archaeologist. "Sorry. Not really fair. Shall we head out there?"

"You're going?" Keogh said, looking at Nate with a quizzical raise of the eyebrows.

"Are you kidding? You see that pile of paperwork? I'd investigate a runaway cat to escape from that."

Nate was driving too fast. He enjoyed careening up dirt roads, right at the edge of control. He usually didn't do it while he was on duty, but it was already proving to be a trying day, and he needed something to make it worthwhile. Keogh was sitting in the passenger seat of the Wrangler with a grin of childish delight on his face as the car sped through the narrowing wash. Dizzy, sitting in back, was keeping a running commentary on his driving like the narrator of a bad documentary.

When he got to the road leading back up onto the desert floor, Nate reduced speed a tiny bit and turned hard. The Jeep slid further down the wash, shot up the road and out onto the straightaway leading to the mountains. He glanced over at Keogh, the archaeologist was still grinning like a kid on a roller coaster. The maneuver had, at least, shut Dizzy up for a moment.

"Why exactly are you here, Ms. Donovan?" Keogh asked.

"Dizzy," she said.

"She's our local expert, I told you that," Nate said as he zoomed up the winding road into the mountains.

"Expert on what?" Keogh said.

"Oh, this and that," she said. "I have enough anatomy to make sure they get all the pieces in the right bag and I'm a photographer, so our sadly under-budget department doesn't have to keep a full-time photographer and bit-identifier on staff."

"Here we are," Nate said. He stopped the car with a spray of gravel. The uniformed officer standing beside the squad car waved when he saw Nate getting out of his car. "Hiya, Greg, how is it this morning?" Nate asked.

"This beats the hell out of chasing drunks, Cap, much safer, more co-eds too," Sargeant Greg Jones replied with a smile.

"Stick to business," Nate said with a laugh and followed Keogh as he led them across the site towards the body. Nate caught a whiff of it before they reached the trench. The body was partially exposed, a black stone sticking out of its throat, the face twisted in a terrible grimace. Nate hopped down in the trench and heard Dizzy drop down beside him. He glanced over at her and she raised her eyebrow.

"Good thing you had the sense to go for the cops," Dizzy said to Keogh who was standing at the edge of the trench.

"Why is that?" Keogh snapped.

"This guy was definitely murdered." She paused, looked at Keogh, then back at Nate.

"Are you waiting for the dramatic music, Diz? How many times do I have to tell you that doesn't work? And what makes you so sure?" he said, baiting her, he knew it, she knew it.

"The same reason the archaeologist was sure, barring the watch of course."

"What reason is that, Ms. Donovan?" Keogh said.

"Dizzy," she corrected him. "First of all, no local culture used this kind of ritual killing as part of their ceremonies, secondly most local cultures cremated, third no local culture used obsidian, oh and that beautiful point sticking out of the guy's neck is a Mousterian hand axe."

"What makes you sure it's a Mousterian hand axe, Ms. Donovan?"

"Get a life, Keogh, any first-year anthro student could identify that, it's an absolutely perfect example of the type. And it's Dizzy."

"Just out of curiosity, what exactly is a moose-staring hand axe?" Nate said, trying to forestall what he was pretty sure was going to develop into full-scale war between the two.

"Mousterian, Nate. It's a tool complex from Europe, associated with Neanderthal man."

"So, you're saying there is a really good chance that it's not a locally occurring tool?"

"Locally occurring tool?" Keogh said. "Do all cops talk like that or is it only you?"

"Only me," Nate said with a laugh.

"Oh, and I forgot to mention, it's a Weston point."

"Diz? I thought you said it was a moose-staring tool," Nate said, amusing himself with the thought of a staring moose sitting on the mummy's neck.

"Yeah, but I'm pretty sure it was made by Karl Weston."

"Karl Weston? The Stone Tool Guy?" Keogh asked. "Well, that would be a break if it was."

"I know!" Dizzy nodded enthusiastically.

"You two want to let me in on it? Pretend I'm a cop and have no idea what you're talking about."

"Karl Weston is an expert in stone tool manufacture. Consults all over the world for museums and universities. He also makes a lot of tools as examples of the type for exhibits and things. He numbers his points so they don't show up in collections as the real thing, so he can track who has them. If we're lucky, he'll know where this one came from," Dizzy said, pulling herself out of the trench. "I'm going to grab my camera."

Nate jumped out of the trench and stood beside Keogh as Dizzy walked to the Jeep.

"Stupid to bury the body," he said to Keogh. "If they'd left it out, it would have been scattered in a couple of weeks."

"True," Keogh said. "If it was me, I'd have thrown him down a mine shaft. Lots of those out here."

"Good idea. You often consider where to hide bodies?"

"Only at the end of a long day grading Archy 101 papers." Keogh chuckled. "Or dealing with grad students. Would you like to see the rest of the site?"

"Sure, she'll be busy for a bit."

Nate followed him around the site as Keogh pointed out the various high points of the project. The archaeologist was enthusiastic about the project and Nate found himself grinning at his explanations more than once. They finally ended up at the lab trailer, and Keogh offered him a cup of coffee. They stood in the shade chatting while Dizzy finished taking the pictures. Nate admitted to himself he was warming up to the archaeologist. Keogh had an off-beat sense of humor and was amusing Nate with tales of graduate school when Dizzy appeared again.

"Lunch? Starving here, possibly dying here," she said, looking at them.

"You say that like you expect me to pay," Nate replied.

"We never pay at the Inn, and I want to try the latest menu item," she added with a wicked grin.

"Oh, no, what has he done now?" Nate was still annoyed by the change in the menu at the Desert Spirit Inn. What had once been a greasy spoon with great Mexican food was now an upscale restaurant and resort catering to a wealthy New Age clientele.

"Santa Fe Quiche," she said with relish.

"First he paints it pink, now Santa Fe Quiche?"

"It's not pink, it's more of a mauve and it is technically Santa Fe Sunset Bisque, at least that's what it said on the swatch. Get it right, Nate. How many times do I have to tell you that?"

"Pink, mauve, it still gives me heartburn," Nate said.

"I think it's the beer and salsa that give you heartburn," she smiled. "Not the pink walls. Ask the archaeologist if he wants to go to lunch." She headed towards the Jeep and got in the back.

"I'm standing right here," Keogh said to Nate.

"She's like that, you'll either get to like her or you'll kill her."

"How do you feel about her?" Keogh asked.

The horn on the Jeep started blaring. "Well, I haven't killed her." The horn blew again. "At least not yet."

3

The parking lot at the Desert Spirit Inn was crowded. Dizzy watched as Nate maneuvered his car through the lot and into a spot that marked "reserved for police." In theory, anyone with a police vehicle could park there, in practice, everyone knew that it was the private parking spot for Nate Mondragon and Dizzy Donovan.

The Desert Spirit Inn sat in what amounted to downtown. That is, it fronted the main highway and opened onto the desert behind it, the view out the windows of the better suites sweeping all the way to the mountains rising stark against the eastern horizon. It was that area, the seemingly empty desert, that had transformed the Inn from an average run-of-the-mill hotel to something special and regularly frequented by everyone from bestselling authors to Hollywood celebrities.

The former Desert Inn had been purchased by Matthew Westfield, a self-made type from the coast. He and his partner had hoped to turn the small motel into a high-end resort for the upper-class gamblers who came to play across the river in Nevada. With that in mind he had ended up buying not just the Inn, but the half section available behind it with an eye to putting in tennis courts, spa-style gyms and a large swimming area.

It was during the required archaeological surveys that Westfield hit the jackpot. The archaeologists discovered not only an effigy figure but a rock wall in the arroyo with petroglyphs pecked into it. The figure, while not as large or spectacular as those further south in Blythe, California, or Nazca, Peru, was nonetheless large enough to suit Westfield's purpose. Rather than pay to have the area excavated and continue with the tennis courts, he had the archaeologist write a booklet on the finds, hired a New Age consultant to flesh out the information and turned the former motel into a New Age hotspot complete with spa, counselors, tours and retreats. In some circles, The Desert Spirit Inn was considered one of the most important destinations in the Southwest, falling only behind Santa Fe and Sedona in popularity.

The change from local hotel and restaurant into a mecca of crystals and health food had not pleased many of the local inhabitants. Captain Nate Mondragon was one of the most vocal, and after many complaints and threats of surprise health inspections, Westfield had quietly reinstated several of the former menu offerings for his local customers.

The restaurant was crowded when Dizzy and her companions entered. The hostess waved them through, much to the disgust of several people already waiting for tables. Dizzy led them through the seating area to the table marked "reserved" in the back. It was always there, waiting for Dizzy and Nate should they want to stop in for lunch, which they did on a regular, nearly daily basis.

She sank down in the chair and waved at the waitress. The small woman came over and took their orders, including coffee. Dizzy frowned at Keogh when his vanilla latte now also contained the word "decaf" while he was ordering. He also ordered the Santa Fe Quiche. He claimed he liked hot food and ordered it with the green chili sauce.

"So, tell me, Ms. Donovan, how did you end up running an institute?" Keogh said, sipping his latte. His voice had a slight edge on it.

"Dizzy. And I don't really need to explain my qualifications to some punk Ph.D. who is getting disciplined by his department." *And now I am so glad I didn't mention those jalapenos.*

"Maybe the department changed their politics and maybe this is an honor working here."

"Yeah, and maybe the pope converted, but I doubt it. I think we already established that I know you mouthed off to that asshole Martin, so I know you're in trouble," she said, glaring at him.

"I'm not in trouble," he said, his voice rising.

"You got sent to Hell for the summer, how is that not in trouble?"

"Oh, for God's sake, Diz, knock it off. You too, Dr. Keogh. I am not going to have my lunch ruined by bickering. Got it?" Nate broke in suddenly.

Dizzy turned and grinned at him, "Sorry, Nate. I'll be good, if he is."

Keogh cleared his throat. "How soon can I resume work on that part of my site again, Captain Mondragon?"

"We'll pull the body today, but probably a week, at least, would be my guess."

"Should I close the entire site down? I can send the students away for a week," Keogh said.

"I'm sure they'd appreciate that," Dizzy said. "A week out of a tent is always a good thing. Thanks, Suze." The waitress set her food down in front of her.

"Sure, Dr. Donovan," the waitress said as she served Nate and Keogh. "Anything else?"

"This looks good." Keogh picked up his fork and took a bite of his food.

Dizzy waited, counting silently to herself. He started turning red, then purple. He grabbed for the water. "Did I forget to mention the green chili sauce is mostly jalapenos?" she said sweetly.

"Very funny," Keogh said, still coughing.

"Not nice, Diz, seriously not nice," Nate said with his lopsided smirk.

"I would have warned him, but no one listens to me anyway."

"You sound very sincere, Ms. Donovan, but I am not convinced."

"It's Dizzy."

"You're lucky you escaped with something as innocent as jalapenos," Nate said with a laugh.

"Don't explain, I don't even want to know."

Dizzy took a breath, but Nate cut her off. "You wouldn't know who left all those crosses on the town council members' yards would you? The ones that say, 'What if no one wanted to save your mummy?' Wouldn't happen to have anything to do with them considering relaxing the archaeological requirements in the valley?"

"Nope, don't know a thing about it." Dizzy shook her head. "Not a single thing."

"I seem to remember a similar incident last year, something about signs that said, 'Save our desert and its treasures.' I think you were behind that one, weren't you? This seemed like your handiwork."

"I've reformed. Having you arrest me, I'm a reformed character now. Yep."

"I don't believe you, Diz, I really don't."

"Well, I'll be careful and not get caught this time." She turned to Keogh. "If you wanted to toss your help in, I would appreciate it. A Ph.D. carries weight, you know, at least with those morons on the council. There is a public meeting and testimony tonight. Nate will pick you up and bring you along, how's that?"

"Are you arranging my life again?" Nate narrowed his eyes at her.

"I'd be willing to testify, if it would help. I can drive myself," Keogh said.

"Nah, Nate can pick you up." She smiled when they both frowned at her.

"Diz?" Nate said.

"Nate?" Dizzy replied in the same tone.

"Fine, whatever, I'll pick him up. That way if there is a slow down through the construction, I can flip the sirens on, always fun watching tourists scramble." He laughed.

"Sometimes I think you get off on the power of the siren a bit too much."

The rest of lunch was pleasant, Dizzy admitted to herself. Of course, she always enjoyed spending time with Nate, and Keogh was fun to bait. She managed to get him tied into knots on at least three occasions. Nate started frowning at her every time she opened her mouth, but baiting the police captain was fun, too, and a favorite pastime. After lunch Nate drove them back to the police station to get their cars. He pulled in next to Dizzy's car.

"What is that?" Keogh asked, a slight tinge of horror in his voice.

"What?" Dizzy said, hopping out of the car. "Oh, you mean that amazingly beautiful classic 1965 Land Rover?"

"Yeah, that," he said, looking at it dubiously.

"Isn't she lovely?" Dizzy beamed at him.

"No, not at all, Ms. Donovan."

"Dizzy."

"I will see you tonight, Captain Mondragon, about 6:30?"

"Sure," Nate said to the archaeologist. Keogh took one last look at the Land Rover and stalked off towards his car.

"See? See why I left?" Dizzy said to Nate as Keogh pulled his car out of the lot. "I have heartburn, academics give me heartburn, Nate."

"The coffee and salsa gave you heartburn."

"Nope, academics, never coffee." She gave his arm a squeeze and hopped into her car. "I got the number off the point, I'll call Karl and ask him where it came from."

"Thanks, Diz, see you tonight." He closed the door for her. "Let's get a bite after the meeting, what do you think?"

"Let's take Keogh to Mango Tree Thai. More chili."

"I worry about that sadistic streak, Diz, I really do," he chuckled and waved as she drove away.

Dizzy pulled her car into the lot at the Baxter Institute fifteen minutes later. She always paused for a moment before going in, sometimes it still seemed unbelievable that she was the curator and director of one of the most respected research libraries west of the Mississippi. The large adobe building that now housed the Institute had once been the home of local builder and developer Wallace Baxter. He had amassed a large fortune before a diagnosis of incurable cancer led him to take the first step to setting up the foundation that would fund the Institute.

Dizzy sighed, she still missed him. She had met Baxter five and a half years ago. They had both been caught in a long line at the coffee shop Dizzy frequented, and a choice comment of hers had made him laugh. They had started chatting and ended up spending several hours at one of the small tables in the café talking about everything from archaeology to movies to favorite books. They had met the next day and the next.

After a month of meetings over coffee, he had stunned her with the offer to head up his fledgling institute. Over the next three years they had formed a close and loving, almost father-daughter relationship and she had worked very hard to build his personal library and collection of antiquities into what it had become. Before he finally succumbed to the cancer, he had seen his small project grow into something he repeatedly told her he was proud of.

She got out of her car and walked in, stopping for a moment as the cool climate-controlled air rushed out to greet her. The building was hushed, it had the feeling of quiet that permeated rooms full of books, as if the bound volumes pulled the sound into themselves, silencing the world around them, calming the mind. She smiled at the thought and wandered back towards her office.

She glanced automatically towards the room that held some of the antiquities. Baxter had very good and very expensive tastes and had gathered quite an extensive collection of ancient art and artifacts from around the world. Dizzy was particularly fond of the few Egyptian and Old European items. Baxter knew that and before he died, he found a large tome from the mid-1800s with translations of Egyptian poems and prayers. Sometimes, when the Institute was closed, Dizzy would go in and stand before the large statue of the Egyptian goddess Hathor and repeat the hymn to her. It helped center Dizzy, remembering the kindness of the man who taught her the hymn and changed her life.

Shaking her head at the almost maudlin timber of her thoughts, she stopped by her assistant's office. Mabel Anne "Manny" Nielsen had been one of those chance meetings that Dizzy chocked up to the occasional miracles the universe deemed to toss out. Manny had been vacationing in town, taking a break between her Master's and Ph.D. She wandered into the institute to see what it offered in her line of history research. Dizzy had shown her around and the two had become friends almost immediately. Before Manny's vacation was over, Dizzy offered her the assistant curatorship, and the two now ran the Institute with almost seamless efficiency or at least that's what they told themselves.

"Hey, Manny, what's up?" Dizzy asked, sticking her head in the office.

"Not much, Dizzy. How was the body?" Manny answered, Dizzy had called her to let her know why she was going to be late that morning.

"Oh, you know, all roses and loveliness," she replied. "Nothing like the…"

"Smell of man's mortality first thing in the morning?" Manny finished for her. "There are a couple of calls, one from Oxford." She put emphasis on the word with a wiggle of the eyebrows.

"Oxford? Wow, we are coming up in the world. Or have we forgotten to return a book?" Dizzy laughed. "You planning on going to the meeting tonight?"

"Of course, I thought we discussed that a long time ago."

"Great, I'll pick you up about 6:30."

"I can drive."

"I know you can, I thought we could save gas that way, maybe get a bite to eat afterwards," Dizzy said casually.

"Okay, what's up?"

"Nothing. What would be up?"

"You and Nate always go out after meetings. I get to tag along sometimes, but never—You aren't trying to set me up again, are you?"

"No, it's nothing like that. Nate is bringing the archaeologist with the body in his dig, and I thought it would be fun."

"For me and Nate to watch you turn the poor thing into mincemeat? Sure, why not," she said with a laugh. "Although I think I'll call Nate and tell him he's crazy to bring the poor guy."

"Keogh can take care of himself," Dizzy said with a snort.

"Duncan Keogh? Really?"

"Uh, Manny? You sound star struck."

"Oh, I just read that article he wrote for *Journal of Archaeological Insights*," she said with a shy smile.

"You never sound like that when I have an article published, and my last one was in…"

"Give it up, Dizzy, the guilt doesn't work on me, remember?"

"Right," Dizzy laughed and headed back to her office. Paperwork covered every horizontal and even several vertical surfaces. Books lay scattered about, some holding papers down, others held open by a variety of heavy objects. She sank down behind the desk, quickly looked up the number she wanted and dialed.

"Karl Weston," a deep voice answered.

"Hi, Karl, it's Dizzy."

"How is my favorite maverick these days?"

"Neck deep in shit, as always. I was wondering if you could look up something for me?"

"For you, anything," he said.

"Your Mousterian hand axe, number 22753," she read the numbers off the note she had taken at the site.

"Sure, hang on, should I ask or let it slide?"

"Slide for now, I'll tell all later." It was a game they played, depending on who was asking.

She waited as she heard his fingers clicking on the computer keys. "That one should be in the museum in Dryland, Arizona. They wanted it for some display they were doing. A museum that size should really focus on local archaeology," he said, drawing a deep breath.

"Thanks, Karl," she said, cutting off the diatribe she knew was coming.

"Sure, Dizzy, anytime." She could hear the smile in his voice as she broke the connection.

By her reckoning, she had heard the American museums for American antiquities lecture 165.6 times. The point six was from once when he was interrupted by another call. She really wasn't into the mood for it today. Dizzy grabbed the rolodex and ran her fingers through it and located the number of the museum in Dryland.

"This is Dr. Donovan from the Baxter Institute, I need to speak with someone about one of your exhibits," she said to the girl who answered the phone. She sounded about sixteen. Dizzy waited while she was transferred.

"This is Lori Hughes," a woman said after a few minutes on hold.

"This is Dr. Donovan. I have a question about one of your exhibits, one that would have contained a Mousterian tool?"

"Mousterian...?"

"Yeah, a black obsidian biface? Neanderthal man? Ring any bells?"

"Funny you should ask. When we inventoried the museum about six months ago that piece came up missing," the woman said, a little frown creasing her forehead.

"You were missing part of an exhibit, and no one noticed? That idiot director of yours must be paying even less attention than usual," Dizzy said with a small snarl. "Thanks." She tried not to slam the phone down, but she was angry. Part of a museum went missing, and they didn't notice? Once again, she wondered how Jacob Austin, the director, managed to keep his job. She shook her head and picked up the phone.

Nate answered his cell phone on the third ring. "Hey, what?"

"Point was taken from the museum in Dryland, they noticed it missing about six months ago," she said.

"You're fast, Diz. Appreciate it. They're working on getting the body out ASAP, we should have an ID in a couple of days depending on dental records."

"I had a horrible thought, you don't think it's Frank Daniels, do you?"

"Frank? Well, that would fit the timetable of when he went missing. I'll pass that on to the ME, might speed things up a bit," Nate said.

"I hope it's not. I keep hoping he just left Lisa and hasn't bothered to call," she said sadly.

"I like that you can live in that fantasy world, Diz."

"If it is Frank, I'll be okay, Nate. I knew it was bad, I know he's probably dead.".

"I'll let you know as soon as I find out," Nate said. "See you tonight."

"I'm bringing Manny with me, we can all go out," she said, trying to quell the sudden feeling of loss thinking about the body, thinking it could be Frank.

"You trying to set that poor girl up again?"

"Why does everyone think that? I was thinking 'buffer' not 'date' you know."

"And someone to watch the fun. Okay, Diz, see you tonight, drive safe."

"Not seventeen, Nate," she replied. He always said something like that, be safe, drive safe, take care. She secretly thought it was sweet. "See you tonight."

She hung up and looked at the papers on her desk. They really needed another person or two on staff, it was getting to the point where they never got ahead. She casually shoved one pile on the floor. Whatever landed on top was what needed the most attention, it was a method that hadn't failed her yet. She bent down and grabbed the grant application from the top of the pile. She sighed, looked at the clock, and set to work.

4

The traffic was light, the mid-day sun forcing most people indoors as Duncan maneuvered his car back out onto the highway. The desert was shimmering with heat, the solid landscape appearing as if it were underwater as the mirage drifted over objects near and far. He turned the car into the wash and started out of town, heading back to shut down the dig. Duncan pushed the car faster than usual, remembering the drive earlier with Mondragon behind the wheel. He grinned as the car slewed a little to the left then back to the right. He slowed the car to a more moderate pace as he made the turn out of the wash and onto the road that led to the site.

"Shit!" Duncan yelled as he reached the top of the road. A small aircraft was zooming along just above the road, headed straight towards him. He yanked the car off the road. The pilot pulled up before he hit Duncan's car, narrowly missing him. Duncan flipped him off and threw his car back into gear. The wheels caught, then spun. "Great." He got out, his rear wheels were buried in sand. Getting back in he turned on the four-wheel drive and eased the car back onto the road. He noticed the plane still circling as he headed on towards the dig.

Marlee was waiting for him when he pulled into his spot by the lab trailer. He wasn't even out of the car before she pounced on him.

"The cops shut down half the site, what the hell am I supposed to do?" she said, glaring at him.

"Shut down the rest of it, everyone gets a week off, how's that?" Duncan said. He was already covered in sweat, moisture gluing his hair to his head.

"Why?" she demanded.

Duncan took a breath, ready to explain, but something snapped, after three long weeks of carefully veiled insubordination from Marlee and the other staff he had enough. "Because I said so, I'm the director and that's it. How's that?"

She blinked. "What?"

"You heard me, shut it down, send everyone home, we don't have anyone working here who is from all that far away, give them a vacation." He looked at her, she looked stunned. "And you, too, go. Home, across the river, a motel in town. I don't care. I want everyone out of here in an hour and a half." He turned away before she could say anything and stalked off towards the cordoned-off area at the far end of the dig.

He glanced at the police officer standing at the edge of the trench, watching the excavation of the body. "How's it going?" he said, looking into the trench.

"Slow, as always," the cop smiled. "Better here than in town, though. Nice and quiet, almost like a day off, except for the stink," he said with a laugh.

"Yeah, nice," Duncan said. He watched their progress for another minute. "Hey, you want to borrow one of my screens to sift?" he said to the men in the trench.

One guy looked up. "What?"

"One of the screens I use for the excavation. Do you want to borrow one?" He looked over his shoulder, watching Marlee stomp around, closing the dig down. "I could give you a hand, I have a trained eye you know, or at least…" He trailed off, realizing that he really wasn't qualified to help a police investigation.

The guy pulled himself out of the trench. He extended a hand to Duncan, "I'm Chris Riley, I'd love the lend of a screen, and trained eyes are never turned away."

Duncan led him over to where the screens were set up to sift through the excavated earth. Duncan watched Marlee hovering at the edge of the police area, wondering if she should come and talk to him. He ignored her for another ten minutes before he finally went over to speak with her. "Yes?" Sounding very casual, eyebrows up.

"Everyone is on their way out of here, place should be empty in twenty minutes. I locked the lab up, too. Anything else before I leave, sir?" She snapped out the sir, but for the first time, it sounded more respectful than sarcastic.

"No, thank you, I'll call you when it's time to open up again." Suddenly he felt bad about losing his temper. "It might be less than a week, it's only until they are done with the investigation. Your pay won't be affected."

Her smile softened. "Thanks, I appreciate that, losing a week would be rough. Time off is nice. I can get a little more work done on the thesis."

Duncan walked with her through the site, back to her car. "If you want to, send it over. I can glance through it and see if there's anything that might…"

"Annoy Martin? Thanks again." She waved as she drove off.

He wandered back to the trench. He and Riley stood sifting the soil excavated from around the body. Duncan's trained eyes paid off more than once as he spotted things the investigator had missed: a button, a bit of broken chain. Duncan looked closely at the chain. It looked like a piece of a man's heavy gold bracelet. "Hey, does this look like an initial?" he asked.

Riley peered at it. "Could be, huh, too bad the clasp broke like that. It could be a G or a C or even part of an O or U. Maybe narrows it down, depending on who this guy is," he said.

There were a few other small items, nothing much, until something blue caught Duncan's eye. The color reminded him of faience, but what would a faience bead be doing here? He pointed it out to Riley, the man nodded and put it into a baggie. Everything went into separate baggies, tagged for evidence. They were getting ready to remove the body when he finally said his goodbyes and headed back towards town to take a shower before the public meeting.

Duncan was standing in his living room at the large bay window that faced away from the development and out into what he thought of as the "wild." He was watching the sun dipping behind the mountains across the river, bathing the desert in a soft rose-colored glow. He saw a small ground squirrel zip around the house and something large, a coyote perhaps, drifting up the arroyo in back. The cacti were standing in spiky silhouettes in the evening light.

A car turned into the driveway, the lights swinging along the front yard, briefly touching the large rocks lining the garden. Duncan watched as Mondragon got out and walked to the door. He opened it before the police captain could knock.

"I'm early, but I thought we could grab some coffee on the way in. I've been up for about twenty hours," Mondragon said, walking back to the car.

"Fine with me, I've been up since five," Duncan said, closing the car door.

"Yeah, and you run too, right?" Mondragon said.

"Captain Mondragon," he began.

"Call me Nate," the police captain said with a smile.

"Duncan," he said. "And I don't run."

"Well, that's comforting at least. All that health in the morning is a little scary. My ex ran all the time and did aerobics and machines and a dozen other things. Made me tired just watching her," he laughed. "Luckily, she didn't want to move here, so I managed to squeak out the easy way." He pulled up at a drive-thru espresso stand and ordered, glancing at Duncan to confirm the vanilla latte.

"Tell me about the meeting I'm attending," Duncan said as they pulled away from the coffee stand.

"Well, it's the town council meeting, but you're there for the testimony about the archaeological ordinance. We have stricter rules in the Hades Wells area than the state does, and some developers are pushing to relax it down to the state level. Diz is fighting it pretty hard. On the other side is most of the money in town. Developers, builders and for some bizarre reason the head of the museum in Dryland."

"What's his interest down here?"

"You know what a boon it's been for archaeologists, the developers need them to come in and make sure no artifacts are destroyed or lost and then give them the "all clear" to go ahead with development," Nate said, glancing at Duncan.

"I know, in a way it's one of the best things that's happened to the field since the glory days of Howard Carter, Petrie and gang. A way to work without having to survive in academia." He sighed. "Unfortunately, in a lot of places the pressure is almost worse than at a university. Usually, you work outside of the construction season, so it's hot and miserable. Then, of course, there are the continual attempts to bribe the guy clearing the land to let it go."

"Yep, and the idiot from Dryland used to freelance a lot," Nate said.

"Used to?" Duncan asked.

"He's really backed off lately. He's under investigation for some land he cleared for a new development outside of Dryland. Austin signed off on it, but before the developer broke ground a hiker found something there and the whole thing was shut down till it was gone over again."

Nate took a sip of coffee. "He's still trying to get this passed, he thinks letting up on the restrictions might get the freelancers a bit more money, and it's a way to keep the Public Lands officials out of it as much as possible. Although they haven't found a permanent replacement for Frank Daniels yet. He was the local Public Lands archaeologist; he disappeared about eight months ago." Nate sighed. "I think your body might be him. I hope not, it'll kill Diz."

"Why's that?" Duncan asked, trying to take in all the information he had been given.

"They were friends, close you know. Sometimes I wondered but no, they were friends," he said, swinging the car into a full parking lot. "We get a good spot too." Nate chuckled. "Job has its perks." He parked in the spot reserved for him and got out. "Let the fun begin."

Duncan followed Nate through the groups of people waiting outside the council chambers. The police captain made a beeline for Dizzy, who was standing and chatting with another woman. They both turned as Duncan and Nate approached.

"Hey, Nate, Dr. Keogh," Dizzy said. Duncan smiled at her then turned to the other woman. "This is Manny Nielsen, my assistant director at the Institute."

"Hi," she said, holding her hand out to Duncan.

"Uh, hi," he said, taking her hand and maybe holding it a tiny bit too long. He realized he probably looked like an idiot and pulled his hand back.

"I hope you're ready to defend the archaeology of the area, Dr. Keogh," Dizzy said.

"I hope so, Ms. Donovan," he said.

"Dizzy," she said absently. She was watching someone on the other side of the courtyard.

"What's he doing here?" Manny hissed.

Duncan looked up and saw a dark-haired man talking to a blond in a very short miniskirt. She was leaning towards the man, her hand resting on his arm. The man looked up and said something to the woman and then walked towards the four of them. His clothes, his watch, his shoes, everything about him screamed money, and money that liked to show off. As he walked over to their small group, his cologne reached them before he did.

"Good evening." He stopped in front of Duncan.

"Go away," Manny said. Duncan glanced at her, her face was flushed. Then he noticed Dizzy's face was rapidly paling to white.

"I'm Carey Scott, I own, among other things, Golden Arroyo Homes development," he said to Duncan in a "see how very important I am" kind of voice. It had the same intonation as some academics Duncan knew. Thinking they were important because they knew more than anyone else on earth about something no one cared about.

"I'm Dr. Duncan Keogh," he replied, but there was something about the man set him on edge.

"Ah, one of the recruits, no doubt," Scott said, smiling without warmth.

"Recruits?" Duncan asked.

"Come to help her with her silly ordinance." The emphasis on *her* was not pleasant in any way.

Out of the corner of his eye Duncan saw Nate carefully put his hand around Dizzy's wrist. "I came to help preserve the archaeological integrity of the area," he said in his best professor tone.

"Recruit, how cute," Scott said. "Your own little army, Dym. Sweet."

Duncan was drawing a breath to reply when he heard Nate speak, his voice was pitched low, quiet enough for no one but those right there to hear. "Leave, Scott. Now."

"What will you do in this crowd of people?" Scott said, waving his hand at the people around them.

"Enforce the restraining order and have you removed. Simple as that."

"You wouldn't dare."

"Try me," Nate said, still in that soft voice. Duncan glanced at him, Nate's face was set, his jaw obviously clenched, still with his hand around Dizzy's wrist.

"Hey, Dr. Donovan, good to see you," a large man said, approaching from the other side and dispelling the tension in the group.

"Hi, Bob," Nate said with an overly bright smile.

"Nate." The man clapped him on the back with a resounding thump. "Got the answers to all our questions as usual?"

"Of course, I do. This is Dr. Keogh, he's running the JW Powell University dig out of town. This is Bob Carter, our mayor."

"A pleasure! Always nice to have another educated type on our side." Carter laughed in a large, jolly way, grabbing Duncan's hand in a bear-like grip. "Always good to have the smart people on our side."

"Thanks," Duncan said, trying to retrieve his hand, the man was still pumping it up and down in a hearty handshake.

"Anytime, anytime, see you in a few minutes," Carter said, sauntering off to mix with another group, his loud voice carrying over the courtyard.

"Nice guy," Duncan said, rubbing his hand with a grimace. "He's the mayor?"

"Don't be fooled by that good ol' boy demeanor," Manny said. "He's sharper than everyone else on the council. The guy built up a fortune in practically no time."

"Still would like to know how," Nate muttered under his breath.

"Oh, you always think the worst of people who are suddenly rich, must be the cop thing," Dizzy said, shaking herself out of her mood and coming back into the conversation.

"You know that his former construction manager claimed he was the source for a lot of the drugs in the valley."

"I also remember the case fell apart, Nate." She turned to head into the room. "I'm ready to go in, get a good seat for a change." For some reason this made Nate laugh.

Duncan followed them into the large council chambers. Dizzy sat in the last chair in the front row, closest to a table reserved for the town staff. Duncan found himself sitting next to Manny. He smiled down at her, then watched the room fill up. Carey Scott was careful to sit as far from Dizzy as possible. Duncan watched as he turned to speak with another man, before the man drifted into the middle of the room and sat down.

"Meeting time, folks," Carter said, sitting down at the council table. He banged his gavel and brought the meeting to order. He opened the public testimony and began by calling the names of people on a roster to speak. Duncan's head snapped up when "Dr. D.D. Donovan" was called up and Dizzy rose and proceeded to the mic in the center of the aisle.

"What did he say?" he whispered to Manny.

"Be quiet," she whispered back.

Duncan listened to her testimony, his brain still stuck on D.D. Donovan. A smattering of applause brought his focus back to the room. He was surprised when his name was called next. He stood at the mic and read his prepared statement, trying to look official, trying not to sound nervous.

Manny was called, and a man who looked like a Hollywood archaeologist, complete with khakis. Lisa Daniels was called next, and Duncan's eyes followed the leggy blonde up to the mic. She was the one who had been talking to Carey Scott before the meeting. She was obviously well informed, she said she was speaking on behalf of the public, not the professionals, to show there was support for the preservation from common citizens. After she sat down, Carey Scott testified on the opposing side, and another man, Jacob Austin. Duncan recognized the name, he was the curator of the museum in Dryland Nate had told him about. Six more people came forward, most representing development companies, and testified to relax the restrictions on the ordinance.

Once the testimony was over, the meeting opened with the council debating the ordinance and they ended up tabling it for another month. After that, they went down the agenda, Duncan listening, a little bored. Finally, the meeting ended, and everyone started filing out.

Dizzy stood up and smiled at Nate as he came over. "Even worse than usual, Nate, my brain has melted."

"Time for food, meet you two at Mango Tree in ten minutes?" Nate said to her.

"I called Ted, he'll have a table." She and Manny walked out of the room.

"Food?" Duncan said.

"Hope you don't mind, it's kind of a tradition, we always eat after a meeting," Nate said, leading the way out of the room and back to the car.

"She's D.D. Donovan?" Duncan asked.

"Sure, who else?" Nate looked over at him with a quizzical expression on his face.

"Dymphna Dunstan Donovan?"

"Yes, of course."

Duncan shook his head. "I heard she was running an institute or something, I guess it never occurred to me that it was here, you know. D.D. Donovan."

"You sound a little star struck," Nate chuckled.

"Not really, it's just—she's something of a legend, you know," Duncan said.

"I've heard her called a lot of things, legend is not one of them, though."

"I was at Powell U when she was still there, never met her though," Duncan said. "I heard her once. She and Martin were, uh, discussing something. Pretty much everybody heard her, actually."

"Yeah, I've heard about Jeremy Martin once or twice," Nate said.

"Only once or twice?"

"Maybe three times."

"Right," Duncan laughed.

Nate pulled into the lot at the restaurant. It was already filling up, most of the locals showed up at the small Thai restaurant after meetings to continue the discussions. He parked in a "truck loading only" zone next to a bright yellow Hummer.

"Can you believe the mayor drives that?" Nate said. "Yellow!"

Duncan looked over at the huge vehicle. "Nice color, manly."

"Doesn't really go with the country-boy look he tries to maintain. He says he needs it to check out his developments. Some of them are out there by your dig. The utility service road that turns off? That's Coyote Estates."

"I noticed the sign," Duncan said, looking over at Nate. "I know I'd like to buy a high-end home in someplace called Coyote Estates. Coyotes are so dignified." He smiled as the police captain frowned at him. "Not," he finished. Nate laughed with him.

"Well, you know, back east they think coyotes are cute dogs that run around with bandanas on and randomly stop to howl at things," Nate said as they walked into the restaurant.

"Coyotes?" Duncan raised his eyebrows, repeating the Spanish pronunciation Nate had used, wondering how far he could tease the man he'd just met.

"Yep, sometimes the New Mexico comes out now and then," Nate said, grinning at the archaeologist.

"You don't have much of an accent, I did wonder though."

"Was it the Mondragon that gave me away?"

"Maybe, but the Nate kind of led me astray."

"It's an odd combo, I know, but I preferred Nate to Ignacio, it's simpler. Pop was planning to join the Church before he met my mom, so I was stuck with the good saint. As a kid it was a mouthful, and I wasn't the only Ignacio in town, so I became Nate. I like it. Gotta say it drives me nuts when people call me Iggy."

"That would be annoying," Duncan agreed as they reached the table where Dizzy and Manny were sitting.

"What's annoying?" Dizzy said, frowning at him.

"When people call me Iggy, Diz." Nate said slid in the chair across from Dizzy.

"Right," she said. "We ordered appetizers."

"Did you order dinner?" he said, looking at her with his eyebrows up.

"Nah, thought I'd give the archaeologist a chance to look at the menu before I ordered for him."

"Thanks, Dr. Donovan," Duncan said. She looked up at him with a frown on her face.

"It's Dizzy," she snapped. Nate looked at her with a frown.

"Diz," Nate said softly.

"Sorry, Dr. Keogh," she said sheepishly.

"Duncan," he said, grinning. "Truce?"

"At least about that," Dizzy said. "Oh, great," she sighed. Duncan followed her eyes and saw Lisa Daniels and the mayor coming towards their table.

"Hello," Lisa said in her honeyed voice. Duncan thought he heard a sharp edge under the sweetness.

"Lisa, Bob," Nate said. "Nice testimony at the meeting, Lisa."

"Well, you know how strongly I feel about preservation," she said, edging closer to Duncan, he could feel her beside him, not quite touching but definitely there. "I had to say something, you know. Frank would have wanted me to." She said the last looking directly at Dizzy.

"I'm sure he would have," Dizzy replied smoothly. "Of course, he'd never expect you to get out of bed long enough to make it to the meeting."

Carter laughed heartily and made a little "meowing" sound. "Now, now girls. I think we've got it in the bag, though."

"Just out of curiosity," Duncan said, looking at the mayor. "Developers aren't usually on the side of preservation. Why are you?" He saw Dizzy grin at Nate.

"Oh, well, as mayor I believe in the protection and promotion of the desert and its treasures," he said. It sounded well-rehearsed to Duncan's ear.

"Promotion being the key word?" Dizzy added, winking at Duncan, he smiled back. "You still planning on putting in a museum at the site?"

"Museum?" Duncan asked.

"Preliminary survey showed several lithic scatters," Dizzy said.

"I'm very excited about that," Carter said. "Adding that to the development, it shows how it can be done."

"And gives you a nice tax write-off for the stuff you've collected."

Carter grinned toothily at Dizzy. "It's a way to make sure those things are preserved as well."

"Sure, selling history off to the highest bidder is a good way to preserve it. The survey still needs to be finished. Anyone in mind?"

"It's too bad Frank isn't here to help us, isn't it Dizzy?" Lisa piped up in her sugary voice. She leaned against Duncan's chair, her hip brushing his arm. "Luckily, we have a new face in town." She let her hand brush across his back.

"Down, Lisa," Dizzy said maliciously.

"Why? Is he yours, too?" Lisa purred. "Now that Frank is gone, you need a new playmate?"

Duncan looked over at Dizzy, she was bright red, although he didn't think the blush had been caused by embarrassment. She took a deep breath, getting ready to open her mouth when she kind of jumped, looked over at Nate with a frown and then smiled. "Bite me, Lisa."

Carter put an arm around Lisa's shoulders, clearly indicating ownership. "Well, we better get to our table before Ted gives it to someone else."

Duncan watched as they walked away. Lisa let her hips sway as she walked, as if she knew he was watching. He looked over at his dinner companions and then down at the menu. After staring at the menu for a minute, trying to regain some composure, he looked up and caught Manny's eye. She was sitting across from him and must have been watching him. She looked away, color spreading on her cheeks. The waitress appeared and distracted them all for a moment as she placed their appetizers in front of them and took the order for their meal. By the time she was gone the atmosphere had changed considerably and they settled into light conversation.

About halfway through their dinner he heard Nate swear under his breath, looking up and following the police captain's glance, he saw Carey Scott and Jacob Austin walk into the restaurant. Scott smirked and walked to the far side of the room.

"Diz?" Nate said quietly.

"I'm okay, Nate, it's a very public place. He won't come over now."

"What's he doing with that asshole from Dryland?" Manny snapped.

"Carey is a collector, you know that, Manny," Dizzy said, defensively. "He's probably hoping Austin can help identify something on eBay or something like that. He lives in fear of getting ripped off, of someone cheating him." She stopped, paling, swallowed and stood. "Excuse me, I need to powder." She walked away from the table, Manny leapt up to follow.

"Nothing like a nice quiet summer in Hell, isn't there?" Nate said. His eyes had followed Dizzy's progress across the room and only turned back when she disappeared behind the ladies' room door.

"Well, it was quiet until today. Very," Duncan said. "I'd like to go out to the site tomorrow, if it's okay with you? I want to grab a few items out of the lab and bring them into town. I know they look like rocks to most people, but I found several micro-petroglyphs that could indicate a cultural variant..." He broke off, laughing at himself. "Uh, sorry."

"No worries," Nate said. "I'm used to catching every third word. As long as I got 'rock, lab and town,' I'm happy. And I'll save you the red tape and take you out there. I'll pick you up at eight?"

"Sure, thanks," Duncan said.

"Damn him," Nate said, looking up. Dizzy and Manny were coming back to the table. Dizzy still looked pale, and it seemed her makeup had been recently reapplied. She sat back down at the table. "Diz?"

She gave him a shaky smile. "Can we have the coconut custard with mangos? That sound good to everyone?" Even though Duncan hardly knew her, he could hear the "drop it" in her tone.

"Sounds good." Nate waved the waitress over and ordered the custard.

They talked about general topics, and then the conversation turned to movies. Dizzy launched into a long-winded condemnation of the recent movie *The Iliad Adventure*. Manny rolled her eyes and

Nate sighed. It was obviously a regular topic. *And she knows it drives them nuts,* he thought, noticing the sparkle in her eye. "I don't know, I thought the depiction of…" he started.

"The depiction of what? Historical or archaeological inaccuracies, Keogh? Are you blind or are you so tied up in your specialty that you can't recognize a trireme without oars? Hmm?" He realized she was grinning at him.

"There is some evidence that the sail could have been employed at that time of year. And perhaps the slaves were taking a break from rowing?" he said innocently.

Dizzy looked at him, he felt Nate and Manny's eyes on him, and suddenly Dizzy started laughing. There was nothing coy or feminine in her huge explosive laughter, it was infectious, however, and the whole table was laughing within seconds, other diners turning to stare at them. When they noticed Dizzy, most shook their heads and turned back to their plates. By the time dessert had come and gone, Duncan was exhausted, he'd been up for nearly nineteen hours and sparring with Dizzy took a lot of energy. Nate finally took pity on him, and they left the restaurant about eleven, Nate walking Dizzy and Manny to her car before driving Duncan home.

"I'll be back at eight," Nate said as Duncan got out of the car.

"I'll try and be conscious."

"Yep, me too." Nate laughed as he pulled away. Duncan watched the car wind up the hill before heading into the house, sighing happily as the cooled air embraced him as he walked in the door.

5

The music of electric guitars started creeping into Nate's awareness. Over the sound of the alarm, he could hear the wheezing of the swamp cooler in the hall. When the radio announcer came on and gave the 7:15 weather report, Nate turned a disbelieving eye to the clock radio. Somehow, he'd manage to sleep through an hour of the Eric in the Morning Show. Eric made a joke about the devil vacationing in Hades Wells. Again. Every morning of every day of every summer he made the joke. Nate occasionally fantasized about arresting him for it. Although he wasn't sure there was a law against it.

He rolled out of bed with a groan, his neck sore from sleeping in one position most of the night. Nate staggered into the kitchen and stuck the remains of yesterday's coffee in the microwave before heading into the shower. Feeling refreshed, he grabbed the coffee and managed to get on the road by 7:45.

It was a little after eight when he pulled up in front of the archaeologist's house. Deciding against using the horn in the quiet neighborhood, he got out and rapped on the door. Not getting a response, he leaned on the doorbell, hearing it buzz in the house. A minute later the door was pulled open, and a disheveled Duncan peered blearily out the door at him.

"Sorry, come in," Duncan said. "I, uh...There's coffee in the kitchen. I'll be ready in a minute, okay?"

"Take your time. Shower if you need to," Nate said, stepping into the house. "As long as there's coffee, I'll be fine." He followed Duncan into the kitchen, accepted the coffee mug, and poured himself a cup. Nate wandered into the living room, idly looking around. He stopped by the desk, it was neat, a paper entitled "The

Microlithic Petroglyph as Sub-variant of Diverse Cultural Norms: An analysis of evidence and new dating proposals" sat on top of a stack of papers. The text had been edited in a bold hand using green ink.

He walked over to the bookshelves, running his eyes over the titles, mostly scholarly. Nate was about to give up when he found the complete works of Gary Larson. He pulled the heavy first volume down and settled in a chair to prowl through the book.

"Sorry about that, for some reason my alarm didn't get me up," Duncan said, coming into the room about ten minutes later.

"I had the same problem. Eric in the morning finally perked into my brain about seven."

"I hate that guy," Duncan said.

"Me too! Let's go and get coffee so we can be out of town before it starts warming up."

"It's already ninety-five outside, and didn't you have a cup of coffee?"

"Yeah, ninety-five and it's only 8:30," Nate said. "And as for the coffee? Do you really expect my heart to keep beating on only two cups? Because if you do, I hope you know CPR."

"Well, luckily I do, but I think we'll try sticking with the coffee." Duncan laughed as he got in the car.

Nate headed down the hill into town to the coffee shop. They were fairly busy, commuters at the drive through waiting for their orders. Nate pulled into the loading zone, and they went in to order their coffee. They were back on the road ten minutes later heading out of town.

Pulling onto the wash road, he debated whether or not he should drive the way he usually did off duty. With a shrug, he pushed the accelerator down, and the gravel flew out from under the tires as the Jeep tore up the road. Duncan laughed from the passenger seat. Nate felt a grin start on his face. The car shot up onto the desert, slewing into the bank before tearing down the road, Nate glanced over at Duncan, the archaeologist was grinning from ear to ear.

"I might enjoy that a bit too much," Nate said with a laugh.

"I might, too." Duncan laughed. "I tried it in my car, but I'm not as good a driver."

"I'll take you out sometime when we have more time. If I can ever escape paperwork, that is."

Nate angled the car beside the cruiser parked in front of the lab trailer at the site. "Wonder where Greg is," he said to Duncan.

"Restroom?"

"Yeah, probably." Nate hopped out of the car, took a step and stopped. He had the oddest sense that something was wrong. He wasn't sure what, but something was definitely wrong. He eased the gun out of his holster.

"Duncan?" he said quietly, his voice barely more than a whisper.

"What?" Duncan answered in the same soundless tone.

"Stay here for a minute, okay?"

Duncan nodded and Nate walked past the cruiser. Something was wrong. Years of being a cop told him something was wrong. He kept one shoulder against the trailer, aware of Duncan waiting at the car. When he reached the door, he turned the knob. It turned in his hand. Nate glanced back at Duncan and mouthed "Unlocked?" Duncan shook his head in an emphatic "No." He still hadn't seen Greg. Glancing around the edge of the trailer to make sure there was no one there, he slid the gun into its holster and gestured for Duncan to come up with him.

"What is it?" Duncan said, still with his voice pitched low. Somehow the silence of the desert seemed to be pressing in on them both.

"I have a bad feeling. You sure you locked the trailer?"

"Absolutely, I actually got about halfway back to town, then turned around to double check, and you say it's unlocked now?" Duncan asked with a frown.

Nate nodded. "We'll check it out in a minute. I want to look around more." He stepped away from the trailer and headed towards the trench where they found the body, the bright police tape fluttering in the breeze. When he looked over the edge of the trench, he stopped for an instant before dropping in.

"Shit," he said as he knelt by the bloody body. He put a hand on Greg's neck, feeling for a pulse. A noise at the edge of the trench drew his attention. Duncan was looking down at him, horror in his eyes. "He's alive," Nate said to Duncan. "Wait with him, I'll be right back."

Nate pulled himself out of the trench and ran back to his Jeep, calling it in as he ran, requesting rescue and another unit. He grabbed a blanket out of the backseat and headed back. Sirens were already echoing off the mountains when he dropped back down into it. He laid the blanket over Greg, not sure how long it had been, but covering him to keep the flies away was something he could do. Nate looked up at Duncan. The archaeologist met his eyes in a wide horrified stare.

"We'll check the lab as soon as rescue gets here," Nate said.

"Yeah," Duncan looked green. "Uh…" He suddenly stood and jumped up, out of the trench. A second later Nate heard him vomiting.

The sirens were close. He could hear the rescue vehicles on the road, coming fast. Nate pulled himself out of the trench to show them the way. Duncan was standing in the shade of the awning, still looking sick, trembling even in the heat. Nate waved at the EMTs and went to stand beside Duncan.

"You okay?"

"No. Whoever did that to him…"

"Yeah, he's a sick bastard, whoever he is. I'll go check out the trailer."

"No," Duncan said, giving himself a little shake. "I know where everything was, I can tell if something's missing."

Nate walked back to the edge of the trench. The medics had Greg on the stretcher and were preparing to lift him out. Nate watched them maneuver the stretcher up and back across the site. They were loading it into the ambulance when two cruisers tore up the road and into the site, coming to a sliding stop.

"Cap?" Sergeant Jack Woods said as he got out of the first cruiser. "Dispatch said…"

"Sorry, Jack," Nate said, walking over to him. "It's Greg. You want to follow the ambulance in?"

"You need me out here?" Woods said, looking around the site.

"I can manage," Nate said.

"Thanks, Cap." Woods slid back into the car. "I'll let you know," he said out the window as he pulled out of the site.

"We found him in the trench. His car looked undisturbed," Nate said to the two men getting out of the other cruiser.

"Right, we're on it, Cap."

"Thanks. I'm going to check the trailer. Owner said he locked it when he left, it's unlocked now." Nate walked back over to the trailer. "You ready?" Duncan nodded, still looking a little green.

Nate opened the door and heard Duncan gasp as the archaeologist got a good look inside the lab. Looking in, Nate could see papers scattered on the floor. There was broken glass to the left of the door. It looked like the remains of a mug, a stain beneath the pieces indicated it had been filled with coffee when it was dropped.

"Can I go in?" Duncan said, his voice sounding hoarse.

"We need to photograph the scene. Can you tell if anything is missing from here?"

Duncan stepped onto the top step and looked in. Nate watched as Duncan's eyes moved around the trailer. "What?" he said when he heard Duncan groan.

"That cupboard?" Duncan pointed to an open cabinet. "It had a couple of pots in it, some tools and a sandal, all excavated from the site. The pots were unbroken, first of their kind found unbroken in this area, at least from that culture. The sandal was rare, yucca fiber, and the tools were of imported chert, we found the..." Duncan paled and jumped off the steps. Nate followed him as he sprinted through the site. Duncan stopped by a large hole in the ground. Tire tracks were on one side of it and a drag mark ran for several yards. "The core," Duncan said, sounding even sicker than before.

"What?" Nate said, trying to conjure the image of what had been there the day before when Duncan had given him a tour of the site. "Wait, that big rock, right?"

"Wow, you remembered, impressive."

"Good memory helps with the job. What about the rock?"

"It was petrified wood, a unique piece, the material was imported, nothing like it has been found around here before, and it was actively used over many generations, judging by the patina. And now it's gone."

"Would it be worth something?" Nate said, wondering at the thefts.

"There are collectors for everything, you know. Problem is the size, you know."

"Cap?" One of the cops walked over to them.

"Yeah, Jeff?"

"Found something you should see," he said.

Nate trailed behind the other cop as he walked across the site. Jeff stopped about two yards from the trench. "Meth," he said, pointing to a scatter on the ground.

"Any of your kids use this shit?" Nate said to Duncan.

"Not that I know of," Duncan said, looking Nate in the eyes. "Pot, yeah, booze, yeah, not this."

"Okay." Nate sighed. "Someone took something big out over there," he said, pointing towards the hole. "We're going to look around some more."

They spent another three hours at the site. Duncan discovered more and more disturbances. Nate followed him as he wandered from place to place. They found several other spots where objects had been removed, the archaeologist looking more and more distressed with each discovery. Nate also located another place where tire tracks led off into the desert.

Duncan had finally given up and sank down at the table under the awning, his head in his hands. "They knew what they were doing, Nate. Whoever they were knew what they were looking for, they knew what was valuable." He sighed. "Hey." Duncan reached under the table and dragged out a small shoebox. He opened the lid. "Thank god."

"What's that?" Nate looked into the box, it was filled with small pebbles.

"A large part of what I'm working on," he said, smiling in relief. "They missed it."

Duncan stood, box in hands, as Nate went to check in before he left. He reported the additional thefts. Duncan had walked to the edge of the trailer, Nate joined him, and they were standing there when a small aircraft zoomed by, hugging the ground, then pulled off, turning before heading across the valley.

"Cactus whumping," Nate said, shaking his head.

"What?"

"Well, it doesn't really work all that well in a prop job like that, but they try it anyway. Jet pilots from the airbase up by Vegas like to come down and fly right on the deck."

"Whumping the vegetation along the way?" Duncan said with a laugh. "Some jerk nearly ran me off the road yesterday. I know they practiced strafing out here during World War Two. We found a bunch of cartridge shells over at the edge of the site."

"Fun times," Nate said, walking back to the car. "I need more coffee."

"Heart starting to give out?"

"Yep, if we don't hurry, I could be dead before we get there."

Nate stopped before turning onto the highway debating for a minute. "Do you mind if I swing by the office before taking you home?"

"No, that's fine," Duncan said.

"Thanks." Nate turned into town, stopping at the small espresso stand at the edge of the highway. He picked up an extra coffee for Sal before heading into the office. She looked up when he put the coffee on her desk, her face streaked with tears.

"Greg?" Nate said.

"Jack called, he's still alive, but in a coma. He lost a lot of blood."

"I know," Nate said, patting her on the shoulder. "I found him."

"Oh," she said, her voice full of tears. "The medical examiner called, wants to talk to you."

"Thanks." Nate opened his office door and ushered Duncan inside. "Let me make this call." Duncan nodded as Nate picked up the phone and dialed the ME's direct line.

"What?" Jim Edwards snapped as he answered the phone.

"Not enough coffee, Jim?" Nate asked.

"No coffee," Edwards growled. "Damn doctor said it was bad for my heart. My wife has been feeding me decaf and has everyone in on it. I can't even get real coffee at the coffee stand down the road. I don't know how she managed it."

"I'll send you some beans, I'll mark them decaf, how's that?"

"You are a kind man, Nate, I'd be eternally grateful."

"Sal said you called?"

"Yeah, got a preliminary for you. You called it right, dental records match up with Frank Daniels."

"And?" Nate said, sensing hesitation in the other man.

"Well, I'm not done yet," Edwards said.

"What? Out with it, Jim."

"He was a friend of yours, wasn't he?"

"Out with it, Jim."

"Okay, sorry. It looks like he was tortured before he died, not a lot of soft tissue left, but what's there shows signs that someone used a knife on him, sharp too, a couple of his ribs have what look like butcher's cuts on them. It would be consistent with that obsidian tool that was shoved into his neck. That stuff is so sharp it can cut deep before the body even registers the pain. I'll have more in a day or two."

"Thanks," Nate said, hanging up the phone. He looked over at Duncan. "It's the Public Lands archaeologist, Frank Daniels."

"And?" Duncan said. "There's more, I can tell."

"Jim said he thinks he was butchered."

Duncan nodded. "With the Mousterian hand-axe? That makes sense, it could easily be used for that, and obsidian is sharp. I once watched an anthropologist butcher a…What?" He stopped, looking at Nate.

"That's what he thinks happened, I mean, that Frank was butchered before he died."

"Like the cop?"

"Just like Greg." Nate sighed. "God, how am I going to tell Diz? The least I can do is tell her in person. We'll drop the stuff from your lab off at the Institute before I take you home, how's that?" Nate stood and led the way back to his Jeep.

6

It was still early in the day. The lot at the Institute was empty except for a roadrunner wandering across the parking spaces when Dizzy pulled into her spot. The small cactus garden was bathed in the early sun, a glimmer of dew still sparkling on the edge of an ocotillo. As she walked up to the door the roadrunner zipped past her, a small lizard in its beak.

The building was quiet; Manny wasn't due in for another half an hour, so the place was silent except for the air conditioner. Dizzy walked through to the small museum, checking that everything was still there. There had been a string of thefts at museums in the area, and it was enough to worry her.

She paused by one piece, looking at it, the way the light played on the golden surface. It was hers, a gift from Carey Scott. She had considered throwing it out—or donating it to another museum, she hadn't got as far as making the calls. She sighed as she walked towards her office. It had been a serial argument when they were together: she despised antiquities collectors and Scott had been obsessed with it.

The phone started ringing as she opened her office door. She laughed, it always looked like it had been ransacked by thieves. She grabbed the phone right before it went to voicemail.

"Baxter Institute," she said, sitting down behind her desk and flipping on the laptop.

"Doctor Donovan?"

"Yes," she said, trying to place the voice.

"Hi, it's Mike Simpson from the Desert Historical District."

"Hey, Mike, what can I do for you?"

"Well, we got a call yesterday from a hiker out on the edge of the public land, he claimed there was some pottery that he said, and I quote, 'looked pretty freaking old' and we were wondering…"

"If I'd be willing to go out and check it for you?" Dizzy offered, chuckling.

"If you don't mind," Simpson said.

"No problem, I'll go this afternoon, desert should be empty by then, makes it easier."

"Thanks," Simpson said. He gave her the map coordinates the hiker had given him before he hung up.

The coordinates were out by the Powell U dig. Keogh would be helpful, he might know some hiding spots better than she did—and an extra set of eyes was always handy. She picked up the phone. The line was dead. Resisting the urge to throw the phone across the room, she placed the receiver carefully back on the cradle. She got up and paced out the door towards the front of the building where the incoming phone line was. At least once a month the phones decided to die. Manny was walking in as Dizzy got there.

"Phones are out," she grumbled.

"Good morning, Dizzy."

"Sorry, good morning, phones are out."

"Keeps it quiet so you can get through some of that paperwork."

"Yeah, I know, that's why I'm pissed," Dizzy said, laughing. She walked to the box for the phones. Everything looked okay, it was at the company's end again. She wandered back to her office and sat down in front of the pile of papers. She sighed and started in on a grant application.

"Hey." Nate's voice broke into her concentration some hours later. The phones had started working and had been ringing off and on, although Manny had fielded most of the calls.

"Hey, I was about to die, you saved me." She stood up and stretched. "We should go get a bite." She stopped. "What?" She could see that something was wrong.

Nate swallowed and ran a hand through his short hair. "Diz…"

"Out with it, Nate."

"God, I'm sorry Diz, the body—it's Frank," Nate said quietly, his eyes concerned.

She tried to fight back tears. "Frank?" Her voice sounded broken, even to her. Nate stepped around the desk. "They're sure?" She could feel tears on her face.

"Yeah, dental matched up."

"Damn it, Nate," she said. "I knew, you know, but somehow..." She was trying not to break down in front of him.

"Diz?" He pulled her gently into his arms, she let the tears go. "It's okay."

"How'd he die?" she said, pulling away and wiping the tears off her face.

"Jim's not sure yet, probably the moose-staring thing in his neck," Nate said, leaning against her desk.

She laughed. "Mousterian, Nate, and that would kill him." She swallowed down the lump in her throat. "I got a call from the DHD, they want me to go and check out the report of a 'pretty freaking old' pot outside of town. Want to give me a police escort?"

"I'm going to lose my job one day with all the police escorts," he laughed, she could tell he was trying to lighten the atmosphere. "I'm sorry, Diz, I can't, not today," he said, growing serious again.

"What, Nate? It's not only Frank, is it?" She put a hand on his arm.

"Duncan and I went out to his site to get some things he wanted to bring in for your safe. I wanted another look at the place, when we got there the lab trailer had been broken into. There were other things taken as well."

"And?"

"You're too damn perceptive. We found Greg, he was in bad shape. He's still alive, but not good."

"Bad how?"

"He was cut up. We found evidence of drugs, looks like Greg might have stumbled into something."

"And they, whoever they are, cut him up? Stabbed or...?" She looked up. He met her eyes, then looked across the room. "Oh." Dizzy sighed. "I guess it's not as safe as it once was to be out there alone."

"Yeah, I think I might have been saying that for a while now."

"Shut up," she said with a good-natured smack on his arm. "What is it, Manny?" she asked as her assistant appeared in the door.

"Do we want to put Duncan's stuff in the small safe?"

Dizzy thought for a moment. "No, put it in the one in the stacks. He can put the rest of his stuff in the empty office if he wants."

"Thank you," Manny said and turned to go.

"Manny?" Dizzy said, winking at Nate. "Wasn't it still Dr. Keogh last night?"

"And it's Duncan today," she said, laughing. "I'll take him back there."

"Kids these days," Dizzy said, shaking her head. "Well, if you can't go with me, maybe I'll take the archaeologist, that way he and Manny can't get into any trouble in the stacks."

"They just met!"

"And that will stop them? Ha." They walked out of the office together and into the stacks. The huge shelves of books were muffling Manny and Duncan's voices. Dizzy stopped to straighten several books. "I heard that," she said before Nate could say anything.

"I didn't say a word." He laughed. "Not a single word."

"Yeah, sure, you never do. Never once."

"Maybe once. You are a tiny bit obsessive about your books, you know."

"Am not," she said, smiling at him. He stopped and was looking at her with his eyebrows up. "Okay, maybe a tiny bit."

"Damn straight."

The large safe was open when they reached the back. Duncan was showing Manny the contents of a shoebox he had in his hands. "I think this shows a variant in the micro-petroglyphs, if you take a good look at this spiral?" he said, pointing at something in the box.

"Wow, yeah," Manny breathed.

"And then again here? I haven't seen this before, at least not small, not here." He was pointing at something else.

"Yeah." She reached in to pick it up, their hands brushing. They both blushed.

"Whatcha got?" Dizzy said, stepping into the room.

Manny and Duncan looked up, both bright red. "I was showing her some of the micro-petroglyphs I found on site," Duncan said, bringing the shoebox over. He pulled one of the small rocks out of the box and handed it to Dizzy.

She took the rock and looked at it, turning it over in her hand. Unconsciously she reached over to the desk, grabbed the magnifying glass and looked closely at the small spiral consisting of thirteen dots pecked into the rock. "You found this out on your site?" she said, looking up at him. Duncan nodded. "Holy crap."

"Yeah, I know," he replied with a grin.

"You're lucky whoever broke into your trailer didn't take this." She handed the small stone back to Duncan.

"I know. They took stuff that would be valuable on the market, pots, a sandal—but unless you really know what you are looking at, these things look like rocks. One of my students, first-year grad student writing his thesis on the area's paleo-cultures, missed these. Walked right over them, and he should have known better."

"So, the little black rocks are valuable?" Nate said in his amused voice.

"Yes, they are," Dizzy said. "Maybe not as valuable as an unbroken Mimbres pot, but to an archaeologist they're priceless." She looked over at Nate, he was grinning. "Shut up."

"I didn't say anything." He chuckled. "Priceless, but not valuable?"

"Not a lot of collectors are into these," Duncan said, carefully stowing the box in the safe. "Thank God for small favors."

"At least not yet," Dizzy said grimly. "I got a call from the historic district, someone called in a find out on public land, want to come?" she said, looking at the archaeologist.

Duncan frowned for a minute. "Me?"

"Yes? You are an archaeologist, aren't you?"

"Last time I checked," he replied with a chuckle.

"It probably isn't anything, but we might as well go check. When we're back, let's all go get something to eat. Meet you out front, okay?" She turned and headed back to her office, aware Nate was trailing after her. "What?" she said over her shoulder.

"Arranging my life again?" he said.

"Nope, just want dinner. Maybe the Inn? We haven't gone for dinner at the Inn for a bit, heard they have a filet non-mignon."

"Do I even want to know?"

"Of course, you do. A lovely filet of tofu, wrapped in..."

"Don't even finish. I've only had five cups of coffee, and my stomach isn't strong enough to survive the rest of that description. I have to head in, I'll meet you at the Inn at seven?"

"Sure," she agreed, walking with him to the front door.

"Be careful for me, Diz," he said, pausing by the door.

"Not six, and I'm taking the archaeologist. What could happen?"

"You never know. I have some of my guys posted at Duncan's site, you know. Help's close by if anything happens out there," he said.

"Nothing's going to happen, Nate. It'll be okay. The worst that could possibly happen is I'll drive Duncan nuts, think your guys can help with that?" she said.

"Doubt it." He laughed as he walked out the door.

She waited until he waved before turning back towards her office. As she did, she noticed the big yellow Hummer pull into the parking lot. She walked back to her office, deciding to make the mayor come to her. Dizzy sat down at her desk and waited for the mayor to appear.

"Hallo, Dr. Donovan!" he said, bounding into the office. He always seemed to have a contained joviality, hearty, friendly, affable. She knew it masked a very shrewd mind. "How are you today?" He was also one of the only people in the local government who still called her doctor, most called her Dizzy, with very few exceptions.

"What can I do for you?"

"Well..." he said, waving a hand. "Our luncheon speaker cancelled, and I was thinking that this would be a good chance for you to come out and get a few more people on our side for the ordinance."

"Sorry, not today, Bob," she said, hoping she actually sounded sorry. "I have to run out and do something for the historic district. Promised I'd go today."

"Oh really?" he said, sounding casual. Something in his tone put Dizzy on the alert.

"Yeah, some hiker found something, I guess." She realized he was looking down at the desk, at the map with the coordinates Mike Simpson had given her. Dizzy stood. "I need to get going, sorry I can't come by today."

"It's too bad, I thought it would be a great opportunity." He sighed, it sounded forced, fake. "Oh well, we'll win somehow, I'm sure."

"Of course, we will," she said, edging him out of the office and back towards the door. "Oh, Dr. Keogh, I'm glad you're ready to go. You remember the mayor, of course?" Dizzy said. "He's coming with me this afternoon."

"Oh, good," Carter said with a large toothy smile. "Not safe in the desert anymore. I heard what happened to Greg Jones." He nodded a friendly goodbye.

Dizzy watched him go, waiting until she heard the large SUV roar to life before she headed to the door herself. "Coming?" she said to Duncan. He caught up with her and climbed into her Rover with an odd look on his face. She hopped in the driver's side and looked over at him. "What?"

"Are you sure this thing is safe to drive?" he asked.

"Would you rather walk?"

"Not really."

"Good, so shut up." Pulled out of the lot and headed out of town. When she turned onto the wash road, Duncan looked over at her.

"Doesn't this head out towards my dig?"

"If you follow it all the way. We are turning off at the gas service line that runs along Coyote Estates. That's where the pot was reported."

"Okay. Did they say anything else about the pot?" he said as she took the turn onto the utility service road fast enough to make the car lurch heavily to one side.

"Not really, just that it looked freaking old," she said.

"Definitive dating technique, freaking old."

"Yeah, it reminds me of an article I wrote for the Chronicle."

Duncan cut her off with a laugh. "I read that, 'Solving Dating Issues: A new proposal in terminology to simplify dating in post-Pliocene archaeological sites' when it was first printed." Duncan was grinning. "I remember starting it, thinking—like everyone else—that it was serious, right until I got to the first abbreviated term RAFO and then stopped and nearly gagged on my coffee."

"You don't think Really Amazingly Freaking Old is a good archaeological designation? It's as least as clear as B.C. or B.C.E.," she pointed out.

"My favorite, since American is my specialty, was Pretty Old But Not As Old As We Would Like, Really. It's to the point and gets the message across, although POBNAOAWWLR is a lot longer than B.C.E."

"That's why the computer god invented cut and paste," she said as she pulled the car onto a small side road. Glancing in the rearview mirror she thought she saw a column of dust rising from the wash road before her car dipped down a small hill. She stopped. "Here we are, it's up this wash, or so they said. Can't drive up it though, it's a little too narrow."

"Good," Duncan muttered under his breath as he climbed out of the car.

"What did you say?" She opened the back and grabbed a couple bottles of water. "It's not far, I don't think we'll need the water pack. Do you have a hat?"

"Nope."

"You should have a hat. You wouldn't want to cook your brain."

"Too late," he said.

"Yeah, I kind of thought that." She handed him a bottle of water and led the way into the wash.

Dizzy set out at her usual pace. Duncan matched his long stride to hers. She watched as he looked around, taking note of the wash walls and keeping one eye trained on the ground. He stopped once or twice to poke at something he spotted. They had been walking for about ten minutes when he stopped again. This time he crouched down and picked up the small rock.

"What is it?" she asked, walking over to him.

"Another micro-petrogylph stone," he said, pointing at the object in question. He looked up the wash. "Can't really tell where it came from out here, might have washed out of the mountains for all I know." He picked it up, slipping it into his pocket. "The location won't tell me much, but at least it's one more to add to the collection."

"Every little bit helps."

They walked on. Dizzy heard a vehicle out on the road. She listened for a minute trying to figure out which way it was coming from, the sound bounced off the wash walls, making it hard to guess. She thought she caught a glimpse of yellow cruising on the road. Dizzy sighed as they walked on, her thoughts drifting back to the last survey she had done with Frank Daniels.

"Hey," Duncan said from ahead of her.

"What?" she said, catching up with him.

"Looks like Anasazi," he said, pointing at a piece of broken pottery.

"You're right, here's more," she said, squatting down and looking at the large potsherd. "And more."

"More here, too," Duncan added. "You think it's complete?"

"Maybe," she said. She picked up two pieces and fit them together. "These two match."

"The break looks recent. No patina," Duncan said. "No weathering at all."

"Hmm, I think you're right about that."

They found twelve pieces. After the first few, Dizzy was sure they were dealing with a single pot. She'd also gained considerable respect for Duncan's skills as she watched him comb the wash, finding pieces and identifying them. There was one rogue item, another piece of pottery, brown with a pattern pressed on the outside. Dizzy looked at it, the piece looked vaguely familiar, for all that it didn't resemble any locally produced pottery. She tucked them all into her pack before they walked back to her car.

"An unbroken pot, where could it have come from?" Duncan asked as they walked down the wash.

"A cache somewhere?"

"But isn't this out of the range for Anasazi?"

"It is," Dizzy agreed. "Maybe a cache from early explorers that someone found?"

"Possibly. I've worked on a couple of sites with something similar. One up Flagstaff way with some points that would..." He trailed off, bending over and picking up a small stone. "That's ten from this wash. Maybe we can head up it one day and see where the source of these is?"

"Absolutely! It could lead to the mysterious cache as well."

They were almost back to the car when a small aircraft buzzed along the utility road before swinging out towards the desert. It looked like it was climbing, trying to get to altitude before it got to the mountains. Dizzy watched it fly by. She noticed the clouds of dust out in the wash again. She got in the car, gunned the engine and turned back towards town.

7

The desert was speeding by in a blur of dust and brown landscape. Duncan was watching out the window, trying not to notice how fast they were going down the wash. When they reached the highway and turned back towards the Institute, he breathed a sigh of relief. Traffic was heavy enough to slow their forward progress considerably, although after a few minutes of listening to Dizzy's horn and ongoing commentary about the other drivers, he was beginning to prefer the death-defying drive through the desert.

When they finally pulled up in front of the Institute, he was exhausted, sweaty and irritated. He got out of the car, leaning against the hot surface for a minute, letting Dizzy go into the building ahead of him. After several deep breaths he pushed himself up off the car. Walking into the air-conditioned building helped cool him off, literally and figuratively. He heard Dizzy talking to Manny, so he stopped by the small museum area, walking through the exhibits. For a small, local museum, there were several very good pieces in the collection. One, a gold Celtic brooch in the La Tiene style had a card labeled "donated by Carey Scott" on it.

He wandered down the short hallway, stopping by Manny's office. She was on the phone, smiling as she spoke. Duncan watched her, waiting for her to get off the line. She finally hung up and, noticing him, blushed. "Sorry about that," she said to him. "I was trying to track down a manuscript that went missing. We loaned it to a university, and it has mysteriously disappeared."

"Into some professor's library?" he asked.

"More likely than not," she replied. "It wouldn't be the first time. Hey, Dizzy, Nate and I are going to have dinner at the Inn, would, uh, would you like to go with us?"

"Uh, yeah." He felt a lot like his awkward sixteen-year-old self. "You wouldn't happen to have a copy of Davidson's *Survey of 1913,* would you?" he said, steering the conversation back onto safer ground.

"I can do one better than that, we have the original, the photos are much clearer. Interested?" She got up and led him into the stacks, stopping by a large room marked "Rare Books." Manny unlocked the door and led him in. "We have Davidson and some others here in the local section. Lock the door when you're done. I'll come down and get you in time for dinner."

"I'm sure I'll be up by then," he said, looking greedily at the titles on the shelf.

"Right, sure you will." She laughed. "I know that look. If someone didn't come down, you'd probably end up here for three or four days."

"You're probably right," he answered absently, pulling the volume he wanted off the shelf and setting it down on large table in the room. He smiled at her as she left the room. Duncan sat down and opened the hand-bound book, the musty-acrid scent of old pages flowing out of it. He sighed happily.

"Are you about ready for dinner?"

"What?" Duncan looked up from the pile of books in front of him. Davidson had been joined by several others. Duncan found a legal pad in the desk and had been jotting notes as he read. He blinked at Manny, focusing, trying to come back to the small room after the time he had spent researching. He grinned sheepishly, realizing Manny was waiting for more of a response. "Yeah, let me put these books away," he said, standing.

"If you're going to be back tomorrow to do more research, you can leave them out if you want. This room is always locked, and the Institute is closed for the night."

"Thanks." He straightened the pile of books and then walked out the door, shutting it behind him and making sure the knob was locked. "I don't have my car, if you want to drop me by my house..."

"Oh, I can give you a ride, if you like," Manny offered casually.

Duncan opened his mouth to protest. His brain played several scenarios and one bad memory from high school. He ran a hand through his hair. "Uh, sure, thanks."

"I do understand your reluctance to ride with me," she said as they left the building.

"You do?"

"You've been riding with Nate and Dizzy. I'm surprised you want to get into a car at all." She laughed as she opened the passenger door for him.

"You make a good point."

Manny was a careful driver and Duncan found himself relaxing on the drive to the Inn. She chatted aimlessly about the town, talking about recent housing developments and new businesses, many of the people in the area and the new public library. "More a computer lab than a library" she said with a sniff of disgust. When they pulled up at the Inn, Duncan noticed Nate's Jeep already parked in the reserved spot. Manny pulled into an empty spot, and they walked into the Inn. It was busy, but the hostess led them back to the table in the corner where Dizzy and Nate were already sitting. Nate waved at them as they approached, Dizzy was frowning at the menu, she looked up when Manny pulled her chair out.

"Where've you been?" she demanded moodily.

"I was on the phone," Manny said. "Actually, I was on hold listening to a wonderful rendition of 'Flashdance' played over and over and over and over."

"And you still think you can eat?" Dizzy said.

"I'll try and choke it down." Manny laughed.

"The good stuff's on the back," Nate said, turning the menu over in Duncan's hands.

Duncan glanced down, the health-conscious food from the first page had no room here. Steak, burgers, tacos and nachos replaced the light 'healthy' fare.

"No tofu, all fried," Nate added.

"Thanks," Duncan said. He was still staring at the menu when the waitress appeared. She took the orders for the rest of the table before he finally made his selection. Dizzy grinned at him when he ordered the chimichanga. Duncan started to dread what would appear after that.

"Did you find what you were looking for?" Nate asked.

"Yeah, broken pot, looks recent though, I think someone probably found it in the mountains and carried it out, then thought better of it. At least they left it," Dizzy said, "there was some idiot cactus whumping."

"We saw someone earlier today, too. While we were out at Duncan's site. They pulled up a bit when they saw the cars out there." He looked away.

"How's Greg?" Duncan asked, hoping he'd remembered the man's name.

"Still out, Jack's with him," Nate said. "Jack was his partner for years until he got promoted to a desk. Doctor said he thinks Greg'll pull through."

"Hello," a male voice said. Duncan looked up and saw a thirtyish man walking up to the table, he had another man in tow. They were both very fashionably dressed.

"Matt, Todd," Dizzy said with a nod. "Do you know Dr. Keogh? He's heading up the JW Powell University project. Matt Westfield and Todd Price, they own the Inn."

Duncan stood up and shook the two men's hands. They smiled at him. "Wasn't your site closed down because of the investigation?" Westfield asked.

"Yes, until the cops are done." Duncan sat down again.

"Oh, have you ever done private surveys?" Price said, his voice had a distinct whine to it.

"Once or twice," Duncan replied. He noticed a frown on Dizzy's face. "It really depends."

"Maybe we'll talk." Price gave Duncan a squeeze on his arm. He wandered off to another table.

"Don't worry if you don't want to do it," Westfield said. "We've been waiting on this piece of land for a while, and we really need to get it signed off."

"Sure. I probably need something to do until they clear my dig."

"Hey, Matt, before you try and drag Duncan away, can we eat?" Dizzy grumbled.

"Of course, of course," he said, moving away.

"He's mad at me."

"Why?" Nate asked.

"I refused to do that survey for him. Probably why they made a point of asking Duncan in front of me."

"Why did you refuse?" Duncan was curious.

"Too damn busy to muck around for them," Dizzy said.

"Oh, okay," he said, still unsure.

"Talk to them, although I warn you, they'll want some ridiculous write up about it and the energy synergy or something silly like that. I remember when Frank..." She stopped. "Sorry."

"It's okay, Diz," Nate reached over and patted her hand. She smiled at him.

The food came. Duncan looked at it suspiciously for a minute or two before attempting a bite. He noticed Dizzy grinning at him. The food was good, he grinned back. Nate asked Duncan more about the site, what they'd found and what it meant. Dizzy and Manny listened, Dizzy occasionally interjecting something into the conversation, but she sat staring at the wall for a lot of dinner. Duncan noticed Nate watching her, a concerned frown on his face.

"Well, shit," Nate said as the waitress cleared their plates away.

"What?" Dizzy said.

"Carter and Lisa Daniels are headed this way. Just what I needed, pink walls and hearty har har."

"Be nice."

"Both of you be nice," Manny piped up, looking from one to the other.

"Yes, mom," they said together and started laughing.

"It's good to see you again!" the mayor said, slapping Duncan on the back. "How did your afternoon go?" He had a broad, fake smile on his face.

"Found what we were looking for," Dizzy said.

"Really? Anything else?" His voice had an edge to it.

Duncan looked at him, sensing the mayor wanted more than a simple answer. "A few micro-petroglyphs. I'm really excited about them, they seem to indicate a more wide-spread use of that medium than was originally thought." He was amused as he watched Carter's eyes glaze over. "I plan on going back out there and see if I can find a few more, tomorrow maybe."

"Oh, how exciting," Lisa Daniels purred from beside his ear. Duncan felt her hand slide down his back. "It would be so much fun to go along with a real archaeologist sometime."

"Maybe you should have gone with Frank once or twice," Dizzy snapped.

"Frankie would never let me come," Lisa said, pouting. Her hand was on Duncan's neck, gently kneading. He leaned forward out from under her hand. "I'm available whenever you want to go," Lisa said.

"Time to go," Carter said, taking her hand and pulling her away.

"Fun," Duncan said, looking at Nate. The police captain was grinning at him.

"Lisa is poison," Dizzy said.

"Yes," Manny hissed.

"Girls, girls," Nate said, laughing. "Pull in the claws."

Dizzy glared at him for a moment, then chuckled. "Shut up."

Duncan let out the breath he hadn't known he was holding. Nate had dispelled the tension around the table. Duncan let his eyes wander around the dining room. Carter and Lisa had been seated across the room from them. He saw Westfield and Price head over to the table, all four looked in their direction. Duncan looked down at his plate, listening to Dizzy and Nate talking about some development on the north side of town. He would smile across the table at Manny every once in a while. Several times their eyes met, and they both looked away. He heard Dizzy snort.

"Diz?" Nate said suddenly, his voice soft.

She looked up at his tone. "Carey?"

"Going over to talk to Bob Carter," he said.

"It's okay." Her face paled. "He won't come over."

"Better not," Nate growled.

Duncan looked over. Carey Scott was standing and talking with the mayor. Carter was nodding. Lisa was looking up at Scott with a predatory smile on her face. Scott shook Carter's hand and then glanced around the dining room, his eyes coming to rest on their table. He said something to Carter and Lisa, the three of them laughed. Scott walked towards them. Nate started to stand when Scott turned and settled down at a table with a brunette in a tight black dress.

"Bastard," Nate said under his breath.

"It's getting late, anyway," Manny said, rising. "Maybe we should go?" They all followed suit, the women walking ahead of them out of the restaurant. Nate kept glancing back.

"What is it?" Duncan asked quietly.

"I'm a cop, I get nervous." Nate shrugged. "Sorry about that, it's been a long day. See you tomorrow." He opened the passenger door to his vehicle and Dizzy hopped in.

"Sorry about that," Manny said over the top of the car before they got in.

"About what?"

"Cutting dinner short. Having him walk in can ruin an evening faster than the Black Death."

"Him being Carey Scott?"

"Yes."

"Is it rude to ask?"

"Well, you seem to have walked into the thick of it. Scott was on the town council when they were hiring Nate. Scott tried to stop it, he had a candidate of his own. It got nasty, he tried to bring up something from Nate's past, something that sounded shady, but wasn't. I think that is at least partially why Nate won out. There's been a bit of bad blood between them since then."

"There's more," Duncan said.

"Scott is Dizzy's ex. They lived together for a few months."

"But no more?"

"They, uh, broke up about seven months ago," she said, pressing her lips together. "It was a bad break-up, you know. Nate's a little protective of Dizzy."

"Are they...?"

"What?" She looked over at him. "Dizzy and Nate? No." She sighed. "No, they're not."

Duncan sensed something else there. "Oh, just friends?"

"Yeah," she said. "Good friends."

"What about Frank Daniels? Nate said he and Dizzy had been friends?"

"Yeah, they were, that's when she was with Scott. I think Frank was in love with her, you know, but he was married to Lisa and Dizzy was with Scott, so nothing ever came of it, if there was anything there. He disappeared before that night." And she stopped herself. "Not that being married to Lisa is a hindrance."

"She's with Carter?"

"As much as she is with anyone. They've been together since Frank disappeared. I've heard a rumor once or twice, men she might have been out with, but nothing long term mind you, she likes to shop," Manny said with a nasty smile.

"Okay." Duncan couldn't think of anything else to say to that. "Turn here, my house is at the top of the hill." He realized he was disappointed the evening was ending. "Thanks," he said, getting out of the car. "It was a nice evening." He held out his hand, she took it with an odd look on her face. "Uh, see you tomorrow."

Duncan pulled out his keys and walked to the door, when she pulled out of his driveway he waved at her. He opened the door and walked into the house. The answering machine was blinking.

Duncan punched play, figuring it was Marlee or the university. The phone in his house functioned as the official phone for the dig.

"I'm at the Cactus Motel, let me know when the dig starts back up, room 335," Marlee said, sounding annoyed. He hit erase.

"Hi, it's Lisa Daniels, I would really like to see you again," her honeyed voice purred out of the machine. "Call me," she said and left her number.

Duncan sighed, looking at the machine. The last thing he needed was Lisa Daniels after him. He ran a hand through his hair and sighed again. He erased Lisa's message and looked over at the desk. After staring at it, he decided there was no way he could write tonight. Instead, he sat down on the couch and turned the TV on, he fell asleep to the late-night news.

The coffee shop was crowded when Duncan pulled up the next morning on the way to the Institute. He noticed Nate's Jeep parked in the no parking zone and laughed as he got out of the car. He walked into the shop and ordered coffee for himself and another for Nate, before wandering over to where the police captain was sitting. Duncan put the coffee on the table in front of Nate and he looked up, startled.

"You look like shit," Duncan said, dropping down in the chair across from him.

"Everyone tells me that," Nate said, taking the coffee. "Thanks."

"You looked like heart failure was imminent. Long night?"

"And a half." Nate took a drink of the coffee. "Some days I want to be a barista. All the coffee I can drink and at the end of shift I get to go home and do nothing."

"Sounds like a good career change for you."

"There are days, believe me."

"Do you want to talk about it?" Duncan asked. Nate looked up at him with a frown. Duncan realized that he had really only met the police captain and maybe he was presuming too much. "Uh, sorry. Don't mean to pry."

"It was one of those nights coming on the heels of one of those days, you know? I got the full medical on Greg about an hour before dinner," Nate paused and swallowed.

"What?" Duncan said.

"The torture and butchering—whoever did it must have known what he was doing. I mean, he must *know,* you know?" Nate said.

"Oh, my God."

"Yeah, the ME called the guy a monster and he's not wrong. And then dinner, well after dinner, Diz was still upset about Frank, and that bastard Scott always throws her. I had just gotten home when the phone started ringing." He looked up. "Sorry about that."

"No problem. More coffee?" Duncan lifted his cup.

"Maybe one more, I need to be in the office by nine." Nate glanced at his watch. "Maybe two more if I drink fast."

"Three if you have them put a little bit of ice in them first so you don't have to wait for them to cool down."

"I hadn't thought of that."

"It's the doctorate. It makes me wise." Duncan sipped his coffee.

"At least as far as coffee goes, right?"

"Yeah, that's pretty much it, too."

"Good morning, boys," Dizzy said, walking up to the table. "You're here later than usual."

"Need more coffee," Nate muttered.

"Oh, one of those mornings, is it? How many cups have you had?"

"This one makes four." Nate held his cup up.

"And your heart is beating?"

"The first three had eight shots each."

"Oh, good, I was worried. Vanilla latte, right?" She glanced to Duncan. He nodded and she walked over to order. She came back with a tray of coffee and pastries. "Can't have either one of you dying from lack of caffeine and sugar." She dropped down into a chair. "Matt Westfield called the Institute, he wants you to stop by about that survey, if you're game," she said to Duncan.

"What do you think about it?" he asked, looking at her, trying to gauge her reaction.

"He probably wants you to sign off on it, formally acknowledge that you've checked it. No clearing, he likes the stuff left out there for his clientele to go look at. I did work for him once but then he wanted me to write this pamphlet for him but after I tried to type 'the energies are channeled through the glyphs into the earth infusing the ground with a sacred vibration' four times and couldn't stop laughing, I just gave up. Figured someone else could do that kind of thing for him. He does pay well."

"I'm not sure about writing a pamphlet, but I think I will go by and talk to him." Duncan stood. "I'll run by before I go to the Institute. Talk to you later."

It was getting hot when Duncan climbed back in his car. The roads were busy with commuters hurrying to their jobs. Horns were blaring as the traffic slowed down through the long work zone. He pulled up in front of the Inn, the open sign was on in the restaurant, but the lot was only half full. Duncan parked and walked into the hotel.

"Can I help you?" the girl behind the front desk asked.

"I'm Dr. Duncan Keogh, Mr. Westfield called the Baxter Institute and asked that I stop by," he said in his best professor voice.

"I'll let him know you're here." She stood and disappeared through a door with an Office sign on it.

"Dr. Keogh, thanks for stopping by," Westfield said, coming out. He shook Duncan's hand with a firm grip and led him in. "Sit down. Coffee?"

"No thank you, I've had my limit for today."

"Are you enjoying your stay in town?" Westfield settled behind the desk.

"Yes," Duncan said, wondering how long the small talk would go on. "It's been interesting."

"More interesting lately. Shall we get down to business?"

"Sure," Duncan said.

"We have a patch of land that needs clearing, well actually signed off. We don't want it cleared. In fact, the more you find the better. If you have time, we'd appreciate a bit of a write up, nothing fancy. I have a full-time consultant to spiff it up."

"Sounds fair. When do you want it done?"

"The sooner the better. It's not a lot of territory and it's already been partially looked at." Westfield paused. "We had someone else working on it, but we fired him. So, it has been sitting there ever since. I tried to get Dizzy Donovan to do it, but she won't, and Jacob Austin from Dryland mostly works for Carter or Scott these days. He likes to clear the stuff so it can go into the museum. We want to keep the stuff here."

"Do you have a map?" Duncan asked.

"Yes." Westfield pulled a rolled sheaf of papers off the shelf and unrolled it. He pointed to a highlighted square about half a mile from the Inn. "This is it. Not much, really. I'll make it worth your while, though."

"Can I start on Monday? I have a few things to finish up this weekend."

"Monday would be great," Westfield said. "Just great! Let me know what you need when you stop by. Make sure you come in to eat first. I'll let them know you are on the gratis list."

"Thanks," Duncan said, standing. Westfield shook his hand. They were walking to the door when Price came in. He smiled at Duncan—the smile made the archaeologist uncomfortable.

"Done deal," Westfield said, steering Duncan past Price.

"Oh, how lovely," Price said. "Does he understand?"

"Shut up, Todd," Westfield snapped as he nearly shoved Duncan out of the office. The door slammed behind him. Duncan heard raised voices in the office. He stopped to listen, trying not to look obvious.

"Don't screw it up, Todd!"

"I'm not, but if we can make the same arrangements with him."

"You mean if he doesn't try and up the deal? Or blackmail us like Frank? Let's get him out there first before we approach him about that."

"The conference is coming up, Matt, and we really need that done," Price said with the annoying whine in his voice. "What will we do if...?"

"We can wait a day or two, let's feel him out a little more before we talk about that."

"If that asshole hadn't tried to mess it up, it would be finished."

"Well, luckily he's finished, so problem solved," Westfield said.

"It better be," Price said. "I'll be in the restaurant."

Duncan moved away from the door, diving into the men's room so he wouldn't be caught listening at the door. He splashed water on his face and washed his hands.

"I thought that was you," a honeyed voice purred from behind him. Duncan turned around. Lisa Daniels was standing by the door.

"Uh, this is the men's room."

"I was looking for you," she said, walking towards him. He backed away and came into contact with the wall. "I wanted to talk to you."

"Let's get a cup of coffee," he said, trying to figure a way around her.

"I want to talk in private," she said, edging closer. She put a hand on his arm, letting it slide down to his hand. "I have an offer for you."

"Offer?"

"Well, there is a little piece of land outside of town that needs to be signed off. My friend had made arrangements with Frank, you know. We would be happy to offer you the same terms." She pressed her body against his, trapping him against the wall.

"Um, what kind of terms?"

"Sign it off, no survey and you get $50,000. We can even send more work your way, work that pays at least that well. And a bit more than that.".

"Yeah?"

"Yes." She stroked his arm. "I can make it worth it, beyond your wildest dreams."

"Let me think about it. I'll call you," Duncan said.

"Of course," she said, laughing at him. She fixed her hair in the mirror and calmly walked out of the room.

Duncan leaned his head back against the wall. *I just wanted a quiet summer in Hell.* He managed to get out of the building without seeing Lisa again. It was hot, the waves of heat shimmering over the parking lot like liquid. Duncan dropped into the car, resting his head on the hot steering wheel for a minute before turning it on and heading towards the Institute.

8

The coffee shop was still busy as Nate finished his sixth cup of morning coffee. He was idly watching people come and go, trying to gear up for work, but it wasn't working. Frank Daniels' murder was weighing on him. He hadn't handled many murders, there had been one when he was still in uniform, but since then most cases were manslaughter. He'd seen a fair amount of death but nothing like this.

"Nate?" Dizzy said softly. He looked up. She was frowning, concern in her eyes.

"Yeah?"

"You okay?"

"Yeah, sorry. You?"

"Yeah." She sighed. "You want more coffee?"

"I should have some, my brain isn't quite on yet this morning for some reason." He smiled at her. "But I have to get into the office," he said, looking at his watch. "I have a press conference about Frank at 9:30."

"I should get to work, too. I have to get that grant app in, and I have about seven bazillion papers on the desk that need to be dealt with."

"Seven bazillion?"

"Approximately." She hooked her hand through his elbow as they walked out of the coffee shop. "Maybe a few more, maybe a few less, but it's close." She opened the door of her car. "Dinner? Just us for a change?"

"Sure, Diz, want me to pick you up?"

"Yeah, around six? Maybe hit the Coyote Grill?"

He felt an actual grin start. "Darts?"

She grinned back. "Yep, and bar chips, beer and disgustingly greasy burgers."

"There are moments when I love you, Diz," Nate said.

"Grease and beer—the way to a man's heart." She laughed and hopped into the car. "See you later."

"Be careful," he said, closing her door.

She rolled her eyes at him. "Yes, mom."

He stood watching as she drove out of the lot, wincing as she pulled into traffic in front of a gas truck. He got into his Jeep and headed to the station. The lot was full when he pulled in, the press had already arrived. The first murder in five years was apparently big news in the small town. He sighed as he walked into the office. Most of the press conferences he handled were about accidents or emphasis patrols.

"Morning, Sal," he said.

"Morning, Nate. I poured you a cup. The chief is in your office waiting for you."

Nate groaned. "Nice."

"At least I warned you."

Nate picked up the cup of coffee and took a sip. Nate liked his boss well enough. Charlie Rogers was a good man, if a little lazy. He'd been elected several years before and treated the office of Chief of Police more as a figurehead and political position and left the day-to-day running of the department in Nate's hands. Nate didn't really mind, it was better that way. Unless, of course, Charlie smelled publicity, then he appeared out of nowhere moving through the department like he knew what he was doing. Which he didn't.

He took a swig of his coffee and opened the office door. He stopped inside the door, blinking away the tears. Charlie wore a lot of cologne and had been in the office for a while. "Morning, Boss," he said to the man sitting behind his desk. Charlie stood up, he was dressed as usual in the movie idea of what people "out West" wore— Western style shirt, jeans ironed with a crease down the front, cowboy boots and a cowboy hat.

"Nate, my boy," Charlie said with his politician's smile. "It's good to see you. Are you ready for the big conference?"

The last thing Nate was ready for was a press conference with his boss. Usually, it ended in disaster. Charlie had no idea what he was talking about most of the time. "Sure, you have something prepared?" Nate asked.

"Yes, I do, I'll read it and answer most of the questions, you step in with particulars of the case if needed, is that right?"

Nate suppressed a groan. "Sounds good. We'll leave as many details out about Greg as we possibly can, though, unless asked direct but even then, let's see if we can obfuscate." He watched Charlie stumble over the last word.

"I'll leave that to you," Charlie said, walking around the desk and slapping him on the back. "Let's go."

Nate trailed after him as they walked through the building, mentally preparing himself for the onslaught of the press. Honestly, he didn't like reporters much. He stopped by the coffeepot in the department's main office and filled his cup before heading out the door and across the small courtyard. The town council chambers doubled as the conference room when needed. Nate paused as Charlie walked in, the place was packed. He quickly identified the reporters from the local daily and weekly as well as the dailies in Dryland and Las Vegas. There were other people sitting with press badges on, he recognized Phoenix's daily logo on one of them.

Bob Carter was chatting with Maggie Yorke, the reporter on the cop beat for the *Hades Wells Beacon*. She was frowning in concentration, then, after making a few notes she moved on. As she moved away, Beth Campbell, the reporter from the local alternative newsweekly, stepped to Carter's side.

Members of the press were not the only people there for the press conference. Town officials and some "prominent" citizens were there as well. Peter Wallace and Ross Smith from the town council, Jacob Austin from the Dryland Museum, Bruce Mitchell, the head of the regional Public Lands office, Tom Kramer, one of the largest developers in town, Dan Hill the owner of a small resort across the river with political aspirations in town. And, Nate frowned, Carey Scott. Beth Campbell sat down next to him, and they started talking. Nate had gotten comfortable against the wall when the door opened, and Matt Westfield came in and slipped to the back of the room.

"If I can have everyone's attention, please," Charlie said, stepping up to the podium. He read his prepared statement, thanking the department for its hard work, sadly announcing the identity of the body. Nate smiled as he watched, he had to admit Charlie was good at this sort of thing. At least until the questions started. Charlie was looking more and more confused, trying to field the questions when one brought him to a dead stop.

"We heard there was another attack," Maggie Yorke said. "Is it true that one of your officers was tortured?"

"What?" Charlie was so shocked Nate was sure he must not have known. His boss rarely read the full report on any case. This time it left Charlie standing dumbstruck, at the podium. He actually looked sick.

Nate stepped up beside him. "The attack on our officer is under investigation. We have no further comment at this time."

"But doesn't that have a bearing on Frank Daniels' murder?" she persisted.

"Both cases are under investigation," Nate said firmly.

"But, Captain Mondragon…"

"Any other questions?" he asked smoothly, drowning out the rest of what she was going to say.

Hands shot up and Nate continued answering. Every now and then he would glance over at Charlie, the big man looked sort of green and he was swallowing convulsively. He let the questions go on for another ten minutes before he cut them off. He turned from the podium, grabbed Charlie's arm and pulled him out of the room before he could get cornered by anyone. He didn't stop until he had dragged his boss all the way back to his office. Nate pushed him down into a chair and went to get him a cup of coffee. Charlie hadn't said a word since that question. Nate handed him the cup, the other man's hands were shaking badly.

"Charlie?"

"My God, Nate, is that true?" he said, looking up, his eyes haunted.

"It was in the report I sent you yesterday."

"I didn't read it. I just saw that Greg had been injured and let it go at that. Is he okay?"

"Still out. Jack would have called if there had been a change."

"I… I…" Charlie swallowed again and took a sip of coffee. "I'll go visit as soon as I can sneak out. What the reporter asked? Is it tied to Frank Daniels murder?"

"Probably," Nate said, wondering if Charlie could deal with the news. "Jim said Frank was cut up pretty bad before he was killed. He hasn't given me a final report yet."

"What kind of monster are we dealing with? God, is it someone we know?" Charlie said.

"I don't know. I hope not, but chances are we know them."

"Oh, my God," Charlie said, looking at him.

"Yeah."

The paperwork was never-ending. It seemed like no sooner than one report was finished and signed off and another appeared. The phone was ringing non-stop. Nate was ignoring it, much to Sal's disgust. She had beeped the intercom no fewer than fifteen times in the last two hours trying to get him to answer the phone, to deal with the press that hadn't been satisfied with the answers they got during the conference. Nate wanted to know who let slip about Greg. The department was so small and so protective of each other he doubted it was a cop, so it had to come from the hospital. He was planning on stopping there before picking Dizzy up to see what he could find out. That and see how Greg was doing, and how well Jack is holding up.

"Nate?" Sal said from the door.

"Yeah?" He looked up and cleared his throat.

"Jim Edwards is on the phone. I didn't want to beep you, I was pretty sure you'd ignore me," she said, a note of apology in her voice.

"Thanks, Sal," he said, picking up the phone. "Jim?"

"Hey, I should have a final report over to you later today. I found something interesting in Frank's stomach."

"You have such a fun job," Nate said with a snort. "Well? What?"

"A gold bead," Edwards replied with relish.

"A what?"

"A gold bead, I'll send over a picture of it, looks pretty old."

"A gold bead? In his stomach?" The case kept getting weirder. A new mail message popped up on the computer. Nate opened it and looked at the golden bead, it looked like it had a design etched on the surface. "Huh. Anything else?"

"You know most of the rest, I'm just finalizing it. It's not pretty."

"Never is."

"Yeah, but I have to tell you, Nate, this one made old ghoulish me sick."

"Comforting, really, I feel better knowing that," Nate said, trying to laugh. It didn't work. When the ghouls are bothered, it was usually pretty bad.

"I thought you would. I'll have it over to you in an hour or so." Edwards paused. "Whoever did this was a monster."

"Yeah, I know," Nate said. "Hey, if for some bizarre reason Dizzy calls you about this? Leave out the details, okay?"

"Got it. Don't worry. And don't forget to send that coffee you promised, okay?"

"Labeled 'organic decaffeinated' as always. No worries, it should be in your hands on Monday."

"Thank God, I'm nearly dead here."

"I know the feeling," Nate said, laughing. "Look forward to that report. Thanks for calling."

"Yeah, no problem."

Nate hung up the phone and stared at it for a minute or two before rising. He had enough time to run by the hospital before picking Dizzy up. He smiled, they hadn't gone out, just the two of them, for a while, and he had to admit to himself he missed it. *I wish...* Nate pushed the thought down. "Sal? I'm heading to the hospital to see who leaked info to the press, and I want to check on Greg."

"Will you call and let me know? I would like to sit with Jack for a while tonight, if it's okay with him."

"I'm sure it's okay." He gave her a gentle squeeze on the shoulder. "I'll let him know you'll be there."

"Thanks, Nate. Have a nice day off tomorrow."

"Day off?"

"Yeah, it's Saturday, you were going to take it off, remember?"

"Actually, I forgot." He laughed. "A day off. It sounds like heaven right now."

Bob Carter and Carey Scott were standing in the parking lot when Nate walked out the door. Nate tried to hurry past, but Carter flagged him down. "Nate, can you come here?"

"What is it, Bob?" he said, looking at the mayor, his back pointedly to Scott.

"Can you tell us more about what's going on with the investigation? Find anything?"

Nate looked at him, trying to figure out why the mayor was so curious about the investigation. He could sense something, he wasn't sure what it was. "Can't say anything, sorry."

"How's Greg Jones? Can he shed any light on what happened?"

"Sorry," Nate said, shrugging.

"Surely there must be something you can tell the mayor," Scott said.

"Nope.".

"You having dinner at the Inn tonight?" Carter asked.

"Not planning on it. Been a long week. I am thinking of having a date with my couch and a box of takeout from Bella's."

"Oh, too bad, we were hoping you and Dizzy might join us," Carter said.

"Sorry, no."

"It would be nice to have dinner with Dym again," Scott said.

Nate turned on him, he started to say something and stopped, taking a deep breath instead. "I don't think she wants to have dinner with you. Thanks, though." He nodded and walked away, hoping he could get to his car before the urge to slap the smile off Scott's face got the better of him. As he got in the Jeep, he saw Lisa Daniels join the two men, her arms sliding around Carter's waist as she came up beside him.

During the drive to the hospital, something started nagging at him. The mayor's questions about the investigation, and the assumption that Greg was able to answer questions were beginning to bother him. By the time he pulled into the hospital lot, the nagging had turned to alarm bells. He stopped by the information desk long enough to find out where Greg was and walked up to the ICU unit.

Nate hated hospitals, and unfortunately his job brought him in more than he liked. He wasn't kidding when he told Duncan he wanted to be a barista some days. Stopping outside the room, he noticed Jack sitting beside the bed talking quietly. For half an instant Nate thought Greg was awake, then he realized Jack was just talking, making contact with his friend somehow. Nate walked into the room, Jack looked up, there were tears on his face.

"Cap?" he said.

"Hey, how's he doing?" Nate asked gently.

"No change." Jack swallowed, rubbing the tears off his face. "Sorry."

"I understand. All too well. Has anyone been in? Anyone you don't know?"

"Cap?" Jack frowned. "What's up?"

"Don't know. I have a feeling. I'm going to set up a guard on the door. No one in unless we verify they are legitimate medical personnel or one of us. No one else."

"Okay, and I don't plan to leave."

"Good," Nate said. "Call me if there's a change."

"Sure," Jack said softly. "Cap?"

"I'll put you on duty here."

"Thanks.".

"Sal said she'd come up and sit with you, if that's okay."

"That'd be nice, thanks again."

"Of course," Nate said, feeling helpless. The urge to run out of the room was rather strong, the beeping of the monitor bringing back too many memories. He walked out and went to the nurses' station. He smiled at the pretty blonde. "You wouldn't happen to know who talked to the newspaper about Greg Jones, would you?"

"Oh, no one would, patient confidentiality is premium, you know."

"Someone did."

"No one from here, Captain Mondragon, I'm sure of it."

"Someone did," he said again, more to himself. He asked around some more, everyone insisted that no one from the hospital had let information slip. Before Nate left, he stopped back by Greg's room. There was a uniformed officer on the door, his partner was sitting across the hall with a clear view of the elevators.

When he got back to his Jeep, he pulled out his phone and called the newspaper and asked for Yorke, she was out on a story. He called her cell number. "It's Nate," he said when she answered her phone.

"Hey, I was wondering when you'd call me again." He could hear the smile in her voice.

"I wanted to ask you..."

"I told you, Nate, anytime."

"Who gave you the information about Greg before the press conference?" he went on as if she hadn't spoken.

"What?"

"Who told you about Greg?" Nate asked again.

"That's confidential," she snapped.

"Just give me the damn information," he nearly shouted back, then took a deep breath.

"You want it, subpoena me or something, if not, I'm protecting my source."

"God damn it, Maggie, this is petty. Is this because..." He stopped himself and ran a hand over his face. "Sorry."

It's okay, Nate. I heard it from someone at the meeting."

"Come on."

"That's all I'll say, Nate, I have to protect my sources."

"If Greg's life is in danger, I need to know." He sighed. "Sorry. If it looks like something more, I'll get back to you."

"Nate..." The tone of her voice had changed, softened.

"Sorry, Maggie, I'm taken."

It was before six when he pulled up at the Institute. He was thoroughly depressed. The murder, the attack on Greg and everything else had come crashing down on him about ten minutes ago. Sal was right, he really did need a day off. He paused inside the door, listening to the sounds of voices coming down the hall. Duncan and Dizzy. She was laughing at something the archaeologist had said. Nate walked down the hall and stopped at her office door. She was sitting at her desk, Duncan was leaning on a bookshelf across from her, smiling.

"Hey, Nate," she said as he walked into the room.

"Hey. You about ready?" Nate said, noticing the possessive note in his voice.

"Sure, let me pop to Manny's office, then I'm all yours."

"Been here all day?" Nate glanced at Duncan.

"Down in the stacks mostly." He grinned.

"What?" Nate said, grinning back. The archaeologist's smile was infectious.

"I'd probably still be down there except they turned the lights off on me."

"They what?" Nate laughed.

"Well, Manny came down twice asking if I wanted to get something to eat and I said yes in a minute."

"And how long ago was that?"

"I have no idea. They finally turned the lights out. I guess Manny got hungry."

"Yep," Nate said, ignoring the feeling of relief that washed over him when he saw the way Duncan's eyes lit up when he mentioned Manny's name. "Women can be insistent about things like that sometimes."

"I guess so." Duncan pushed himself off the bookshelves. "Where're you two headed?"

"Coyote Grill, beer, burgers and darts," Nate said. "You?"

"Bella's Italian."

"Good choice. I have a day off tomorrow, want to get breakfast?" he said.

"Sure, call me before you come by, though, so I can be conscious, at least mostly," Duncan said, laughing.

"I'll try and be in that state, too."

"Are you going to shut up and take me out for food?" Dizzy called from the hall. "I could die, you know."

Nate laughed. "Coming." She smiled at him and tucked her hand through his arm the way she always did, leaning against him. He looked down at her, the depression already easing, and by the time they got their drinks at the pub he was feeling nearly human again.

"How are you holding up?" she said quietly. "With Greg and all?"

He looked at her. "I'm managing. It was rough at the hospital. I guess I feel a bit like it's my fault he's there. I know it's because I want to find someone to blame." He looked away. "I feel helpless when I'm there.

"I'm sorry," she said, putting her hand on his arm.

"It's usually okay, it was being back there, you know. It smells the same."

"I know," she said gently. "Do you want to talk?"

"No, I'm okay." He had no intention of ruining his evening.

"Bob Carter called and asked if we wanted to go out to dinner tonight," she said.

"He stopped me outside the office and asked, too. I said no."

"Me too, especially when he said Carey would be there."

"Yeah, well Carter is an ass about shit sometimes, Diz. Let's pretend we didn't mention them and have a nice meal?"

"Sure," she said, sounding anything but sure. He watched her eyes move to the door and then back to his face.

"He won't be here tonight, Diz. He's having dinner at the Inn with Carter and Lisa."

"Are you positive?" she said in the small voice that appeared when she was talking about Scott.

"Has he been bothering you?" Nate said, feeling anger starting to build.

She shrugged. "Hades Wells is remarkably small, you know that, Nate. At least in the circles we move in."

"Diz? What the hell does that mean?"

"Nothing, he shows up where we are, and he sent flowers to the office again."

"What?" he snapped, aware his heart sped up. "Next time I see him, I might shoot him just a little. Only a teeny bit, mind you."

"Sorry I mentioned it, Nate, relax. Let's eat, okay?" She looked up at him, he saw the mood change.

"Okay, I'll let it go, but if he bothers you again, let me know."

"Promise," she said brightly.

They ordered dinner and took over the dart board. Nate felt the tension of the last few days starting to unwind. More than once he almost brought up the call from Jim Edwards about the bead in Frank's stomach, but he let it drop, deciding to leave the office completely behind him for the night.

Dizzy was in a good mood after she beat him three games straight and he happily put up with her good-natured teasing. They ate and played several more games, the evening winding towards night. He didn't realize how long they'd been there until the waitress stopped by for last call. Nate sighed, not really wanting the evening to end. Dizzy met his eyes and smiled, he smiled back. When they left, she let him put an arm over her shoulders and leaned her head against him.

"I have a day off tomorrow," he said as they got in the car.

"Damn, I have to go up to the pass. I promised I would check out the vandalism up there," she said.

"Ah, Diz, cancel."

"I can't, Nate, I'm sorry. Come with me," she said.

"I really wanted to sleep in a bit," he said, embarrassed by the whine in his voice.

"I won't go too early. Come with me."

"Let me think about it."

"And that means no," she said angrily.

"That means I'll think about it, Diz. That's all," he said. He drove in silence for several minutes. "Sorry."

"Yeah, me too." She looked over at him. "I didn't know you had a day off when I scheduled this. I really can't weasel out of it again."

"It's okay, I might wake up fresh as a daisy and want to go," he said. Nate pulled up at the Institute. "Call me in the morning."

"Sure," she said. "I had a nice night, Nate."

"Me, too." He waited until she was safely in her car before pulling out and heading home.

9

The morning sun was starting to warm the desert, dust from far-off construction making the air hazy, almost like a morning fog. Traffic was light as Dizzy drove out of town, regular commuters not out on Saturday, and tourists not up yet. The highway over the pass was empty except for a semi heading down the hill, brakes smoking, the harsh metallic smell of burning brake pads filling the car as Dizzy drove past.

Once she crested the hill, she started watching for the turn off onto the Public Lands service road that led into the mountains and to the area she was steward over. She'd thought long and hard before she accepted the position, but knowing she could help preserve an important site finally swayed her.

She was happily singing along with the radio when her phone rang. She glanced at the caller ID as she pulled onto the dirt road. "Nate, hey."

"Where are you?"

"Heading out towards Windy Pass, remember?" She paused. "Why?"

"Oh, you're already on the road? I thought you were going to call," Nate said, Dizzy could hear the disappointment in his voice.

"I tried, twice, but then decided to let you sleep. What's up?"

"Duncan and I were going to grab a bite, and I thought I'd invite you along."

"How about dinner? I'll bring Manny and she and Duncan can make calf eyes at each other while we talk."

"You think maybe you're a little hard on them, Diz?"

"They're like two sixteen-year-olds, they deserve the teasing. I'll be back in town by four," she said.

"Oh, we got the final autopsy report back on Frank. It's pretty much what I told you. Looks like he'd been buried for about eight months. Stone tool delivered the killing blow. But we figured that," Nate said, rattling the information.

"Thanks, Nate, anything else?"

"Jim said there was a gold bead in his stomach."

"What?"

"He sent over pictures. I want you to look at them, they look, well, old or something. You can look tonight before dinner, how's that."

"Old or something? You should become an archaeologist, you're as vague as most of us."

"Thanks, I think. I'll bring them to dinner?"

"Sure, I'll call as soon as I'm out of the mountains and have a signal."

"Thanks, don't be late, and Diz, be careful, okay" Nate said, his voice softening.

"Always am, you know that, Nate. See you tonight."

Dizzy flipped her phone closed. She made the turn into the mountains, the road began climbing up steeply from the desert floor. The vegetation started to change, chaparral, brittle bush and teddy bear cholla giving way to Joshua trees, juniper and jumping cholla. The air coming in the windows was fractionally cooler as the car climbed. She passed an old miners' shack, the tailings from the mine piled around the edges of the cabin, hiding the hole in the earth but creating a scar on the otherwise pristine landscape.

The final turn onto the narrow track into the pass itself came up faster than she had expected. She pulled into a broad sandy spot that she tended to think of as her personal parking spot. The rocky barren mountains soared above the area, the pass itself a slash down through them, carved by wind and water, as much as twenty feet wide in places, narrowing to less than a yard in others.

Dizzy hopped out of the Land Rover and walked around to the back. She filled her two-liter water pack from the five-gallon cooler in the back of the car. After grabbing her survey bag, she slung it over her shoulder, locked up the car and headed into the pass. Since the day was heating up, she decided to check the rock art, then refill her water pack, and head over to the other sites to the east.

It was hot in the pass, the rock walls magnifying the heat of the day. Mirage was already simmering like a thin layer of water all around her as she walked deeper into the mountains. Dizzy stopped for a minute, putting a small stone on the growing pile of rocks marking a memorial to a hiker and his young daughter. They had ventured too far from their car with too little water, underestimating the speed with which the desert summer could kill. They died there, the desert finally claiming them a mere two miles from their car. Dizzy always stopped for a moment at the spot.

As she moved on, she was keeping an eye on various small sites she knew were there, luckily most were hard to spot unless you had an expert's eyes. The area had been a busy place in the past, and evidence of man's habitation was everywhere if you knew where to look. She paused in the shade of a rock outcropping, glancing up at the petroglyphs on the low ceiling of the small overhang. Two more were missing. Dizzy pulled out her camera and took pictures, carefully zooming in on the places where two drawings had been removed, the sandstone sliced away, as well as the damage the removal had done to the surrounding petroglyphs. Then she moved on.

Movement high above her caused her to stop for a moment. A bighorn sheep peered down a steep hill at her. She waved at it and continued down the water-worn path into the narrowest part of the canyon. She slowed for an instant, fighting back the feeling of claustrophobia she always got when traversing this area. Something about the way the mountains rose above her, nearly touching, almost creating a cave, made her nervous, even after more than a dozen trips through here. It was cooler and smelled slightly damp, a tiny amount of water seeped down the northern cliff face and collected there. It wasn't enough to make even a small pool, but more than enough to create the rich smell of moisture in the dry environment.

She stopped for a moment as the sound of a vehicle echoed through the pass. No doubt, someone in a four-wheeling on the other side of the pass. She sighed, annoyed by the presence of someone driving through the quiet mountains.

Once on the other side of the closed in area, she turned off the main track, heading up a narrow trail to a large rock shelter about fifteen feet up from the floor of the canyon. She noticed the trail had been disturbed. Burros, bighorn sheep and a coyote had all been through recently. As she reached the top she noticed a boot print, further on another. Hoping they had been made by a curious hiker but knowing they probably weren't, she headed into the rock shelter. The southern face of the shelter wall was covered in petroglyphs, the bighorn sheep was a predominant motif, but there were others as well. Spirals, squares, zig-zagging lines and even a coyote decorated the wall. Her heart sank when she realized that one of her favorites, a small family of bighorn sheep, had been removed from the wall.

Dizzy photographed the petroglyphs, the empty spots where she knew others had been, and then the whole area, documenting it again to show the damage looters were doing over time. She looked out of the shelter, noticing the prints of both bighorn sheep and burros. Sipping on her water, she decided it was time to head back for a refill.

She slid back down the trail and was about to turn into the pass when something caught her eye. She walked over to the unusual object lying in the sand by the trail. Stopping her hand before she touched it, she pulled out the camera and photographed it *in situ* before picking it up. The small green stone object was as out of place here as a polar bear. Dizzy looked at it. The piece actually looked familiar, she couldn't place where she'd seen it, but she knew one thing without a doubt. It was Pre-Columbian. She picked it up, slid it into her survey bag and headed back into the pass.

The trip back was quicker, it always was, she wasn't as focused on the land around her, and she tended to hurry. Being caught without water worried her. She rounded the corner at the end of the pass and stopped, panic suddenly rising in her, chilling her despite the heat.

"No!" she said it aloud, her voice echoing through the pass. The Land Rover was gone. Dizzy was looking at the empty place where she knew she had parked her car when the rock face beside her suddenly exploded in a shower of stone. One of the fragments caught her on the head and she dropped, a split second later the crack of a rifle echoed in the silent desert.

Dizzy stayed down, unmoving. Hoping that playing dead was the right choice. She heard rocks tumbling down the cliff face above her to her right. Someone was moving around up there. She held perfectly still, not daring to move, holding her breath as the heat from the rocks she was lying on began seeping through her shirt, burning her.

"I think you hit her," an angry male voice shouted, loud in the vast stillness of the midday desert, distorted by the echo.

"No, I know I didn't, I just put her down, trust me," another voice answered. "Hang on, I'll show ya how good I am." Harsh laughter filled the air. Dizzy felt the water pack on her back jerk, then the crack of the shot, the last of the sport drink running out of the hole in the pack and over her back. "Let's go."

Dizzy stayed still until she heard an engine start up and a vehicle moving down the road away from the pass. She could smell the acrid smell of the dust and engine exhaust as she lay there, the rock burning her skin and the last of her water quickly drying in the 115-degree heat.

"Shit," she said again, pushing herself up. She took the pack off and dropped it on the ground. Looking at her watch she sighed, No one would miss her for several hours. The walk to the other side of the pass would take about an hour. Her phone might work there. She pulled a pencil out of her bag and scrawled *Heading west through pass-D* on the rock, just in case someone came looking for her. Pulling her hat off and letting the breeze blow through sweat-dampened hair, she turned back towards the mountains.

10

The breakfast crowd at the Inn was made up of an even mix of tourists, guests and locals, the smells of coffee, frying eggs, bacon and pastries filling the room. Nate idly watched people come and go as he sat at his table. Matthew Westfield was flitting between the tables, chatting with locals, behaving expansively to guests. His voice carried across the room, the rich, carefully cultivated tone easily overwhelming other conversations. Todd Price was also around that morning, sitting at a table in the corner, watching the room, sipping coffee and looking bored.

Suze, the waitress, stopped by the table again to fill their cups, Nate was on his ninth for the day. She smiled at him with her inviting smile and then turned her attention to Duncan. Not getting the response she wanted, she huffed and walked to the next table.

"Do we have to get that look every time?" Duncan said.

"I think so, every time, she has hopes, I think," Nate replied.

"Great, maybe we can eat somewhere else from now on?"

"That'd be fine, but we eat here for free."

"On the take, Captain?"

"Yep, you can buy me off with free coffee, simple as that."

Duncan looked at him for a long minute. "Something interesting happened yesterday."

"What?"

"I hate to say this, but can we be off the record?" he said, watching carefully for Nate's reaction.

"No record on my day off."

"Someone approached me yesterday and asked if I would consider some freelance work."

"Lots of archaeologists do, I know."

"He wanted to know if he could make the same arrangements with me as with Frank Daniels."

Nate put his coffee down. "What did he mean by that?"

"I asked the same question." Duncan paused. "To make a long story short, he offered me $50,000 to sign off on the land without a survey."

"Who?" Nate said, frowning.

"Not sure if that matters, does it? He did imply there would be other jobs out there if I was willing to play ball with them."

"And he said Frank had made arrangements like this in the past?"

"He implied he had."

"What did you say?" Nate picked up his coffee again.

"I told him I'd think about it, I thought it might help with the investigation, you know. I hope I didn't step too far out of line?"

"The $50,000 wasn't motivation at all?" Nate said, teasing. When he saw the other man's face darken, he stopped smiling. "Didn't mean it, sorry. I wonder if anyone has ever asked Diz?"

"I doubt it, she is pretty vocal about preservation. Did you read that article she wrote for the 'Chronicle of Archaeology'? It all sounded very academic but what boiled down to was archaeologists who behave that way should be drawn and quartered." Duncan chuckled.

"That sounds like her. I wonder if they realize she really means it? I mean the drawing and quartering?"

"Once they meet her, they will," Duncan said, picking up his coffee and leaning back.

Nate glanced at his watch. The morning was sliding away, but he really had no inclination to get moving. Days off were becoming increasingly rare and the thought of a moment of quiet time was almost intoxicating. He was still annoyed at Dizzy for planning the day in the mountains.

"When will Dizzy be back in town?" Duncan asked sometime later.

"What?" Nate looked up. "Sorry, my mind decided to take a break. Diz'll be back in around four she said. She'll want to change, then we can all head out to dinner."

"She's arranging our lives, I think."

"She enjoys it," Nate said, standing. "You ready to go? I have to drive out to the lake, want to come?"

"Isn't it your day off?"

"Yeah, and if I go today, I can take my own sweet time getting there and back. I like to come back on the old mine road east of town."

Duncan grinned in anticipation. "Dirt road?"

"Yep, you game?" Nate grinned back as they headed out of the Inn.

Nate always enjoyed the drive out to the lake. The sudden break between town and desert still struck him. One minute the road passed through civilization and the next it was desert, stretching away to craggy mountains on either side of the valley. Then, as the recreational area drew near, vacation homes began to dot the landscape, solitary islands of humanity overwhelmed by the stark, wild desert looming in, untouched by civilization, on all sides. The small resort area at the lake was green and lush, the smell of eucalyptus strong in the hot air.

Nate pulled into the "no parking anytime" spot outside the ranger station and switched the car off. "I'll introduce you if you want," he said to Duncan. "Ranger here is...Well, he's a character."

Duncan followed him as they walked into the ranger station. Nate introduced the archaeologist to Bill Smith, who proceeded to regale Duncan with tales of all the drunken archaeologists he had known in his long career. It took nearly an hour and three cups of a coffee-flavored sludge before they were able to get back to the Jeep.

"Character?" Duncan asked with a grimace.

"Opinionated bastard?" Nate offered.

"Better. Remind me to avoid your introductions in the future."

Nate laughed as he pulled out of the parking lot. He followed the road a few miles further to the north before he made the turn onto the old mining road. It was a favorite spot, not much used by four-wheelers and a nice challenge for his driving skills. About a mile in, tailings from the mine rose up more than ten feet on either side of the road, the track winding through the man-made canyon with hairpin turns and sudden drops. He paused for a minute at the beginning of the road and looked over at Duncan. "Ready?"

"Let's go!"

Nate pulled the car onto the road, slowly accelerating, getting the feel of the gravel beneath the tires. The first curve in the road was approaching. He took it fast, the Jeep sliding to the left before the wheel caught again and the car shot forward. Nate risked a glance over at Duncan who was grinning like a kid. He laughed at himself, knowing full well that same look of glee was on his face.

They were getting to the tailings, a new rut in the road caught him by surprise and he lost control for half a second, wrenching the car around he went into the "canyon," twisting and turning between the white walls on either side of them. The car finally zoomed out of the tailings and up into the desert again.

Nate realized his phone was ringing. He pulled the car to a sliding stop and grabbed his phone. "Better be good, Sal, it's my day off."

"Nate..." She paused for a minute.

"What's wrong?" he asked, instantly sensing a crisis.

"Patrol car called, they found Dizzy's Rover at milepost 19."

His stomach clenched and he had to swallow before he answered her. "Is she alive?"

"She's not in it, Henry said it had been hotwired, radio is missing, cell charger too, but the big five-gallon cooler is still in back. I tried her cell, Nate, goes to voicemail."

"She was surveying up in the mountains today, her cell won't work there, thanks Sal." He snapped the phone closed and looked over at Duncan. "We got to go."

"What is it?" Duncan said, concern coloring his voice, a frown on his face.

"Diz," Nate said, pulling the car back onto the road. "They found her car empty, looks like someone took it. We're going to head up to Windy Pass and see if she's still out there."

"I'm sure she's fine, Nate."

"I hope so."

Nate reached the highway ten minutes later. As he pulled onto the blacktop, he flipped on lights and sirens and plowed up the highway, dangerously passing a couple of slow-moving semis in his rush to get over the hill. He turned onto the Public Lands service road less than twenty minutes from the time of Sal's call. The drive had been silent, Nate forcing the Jeep up the road, trying not to be reckless, but he had a growing sense of unease that was fast becoming something akin to panic. The car was at the edge out of control as he took the turn towards the pass. When they finally got to the parking area, after what felt like hours, he slammed the car to a gravel-scattering stop.

"Get the first aid kit in the backseat and grab a couple of ice packs out of it," Nate said to Duncan as he went to the back of the vehicle and grabbed a couple of water bottles from the back. He put the bottles in a backpack and took the ice packs from Duncan, tucking them into the pack as well. "Let's go," he said as he led the way into the pass.

"What's that?" Duncan said, pointing at the blue and gray water pack lying just inside the rock walls of the canyon.

"It looks like Diz's." Nate ran over and picked up the water pack. He ran his finger over the hole in the pack, his eyes scanning the pass in front of him. He glanced down at the stain on the ground, flies had settled on the sticky remains. He was about to rise when something else caught his eye, a small, darker stain on the ground.

"This looks like blood," he said.

"Nate?" Duncan said, concerned. "There's a note on the rock, 'Heading west through pass, D.' You think that's Dizzy?"

Nate stood. "Yeah, she's probably thinking she can get cell reception on the other side." He started into the pass, walking quickly, Duncan's long strides matching his.

"Lots of habitation here." Duncan was looking around. Something about the look on his face led Nate to believe he was making notes about what he was seeing.

"Diz showed me some of it. She's steward up here, so we come up quite a bit," Nate said, trying to distract himself from the growing panic. "She was up here today following up on a report of vandalism in the big rock shelter on the other end of the pass."

"There's a lot of that going on out here. I went up to Oak Canyon on a day off a couple of weeks ago, and you could see where people had actually cut petroglyphs out of the rocks. Heartbreaking," Duncan said. "I saw one piece I'm pretty sure was from there on eBay. I check the antiquities on a regular basis, just to see what's come up."

"Diz does that a lot, too. She's crazed about it, in fact. I worry what will happen if she ever catches someone in the act. She can be stupid about stuff like that. What?" he said when Duncan suddenly stopped.

Duncan walked under the large outcropping of rock on the left-hand side of the pass. He bent down and pulled out a khaki shoulder bag from behind a rock. Nate recognized it instantly, Dizzy's survey bag. The archaeologist walked back over with the bag in his hands. He handed it to Nate.

"I'm sure she stowed it so she could travel lighter," Nate said, more to himself than Duncan, then opening the bag. "Good eyes, catching that, I wouldn't even have noticed. What's this?" He pulled a small stone figure out of the bag and handed it to Duncan. The archaeologist took it and turned it over in his hands.

"Looks, hmm, Mayan? Maybe, definitely Pre-Columbian. Shit, I think it's authentic."

"What is it doing in her bag?" Nate took the statue and put it back in the bag. They walked on, the narrows closing over their heads, the air relatively cooler in the dim passage, making the heat on the other side even more palpable.

His panic was growing with every step. It had been nearly an hour since Sal had called. He glanced at his watch; it was after two. The sun was beating down on the canyon, the rock walls amplifying the heat. A flash of color under the shade of a rock about thirty yards ahead of him made him stop for half a second, then he ran, and kneeled beside the prone figure. He heard Duncan come up behind him.

"Diz?" He gently turned her over. "Diz?" He pulled a bottle of water out of the pack and poured it on her face. "Diz, come on." He heard the note of panic in his voice. Something cold was pressed into his hand, Duncan had grabbed the ice pack and activated it.

"Put in on the inside of her elbow," the archaeologist said. "I know that sounds strange, but an acupuncturist told me about it. It works, can save someone in heat stroke."

Nate put the ice pack on Dizzy's elbow, pouring more water on her face, letting a tiny amount dribble in her mouth. "Diz, come on." He fished in his pocket and handed Duncan his phone. "You should be able to get a signal down the pass a bit, keep trying, call rescue on my authority and have them scramble a chopper for the west end of Windy Pass. I'm right behind you." The archaeologist sprinted down the pass, phone open, watching, Nate knew, for enough bars to make the call.

Once he was alone, Nate pulled Dizzy gently into his arms, "Come on, Diz, don't do this." He struggled to his feet, her body feeling light as he held her. As quickly as possible, he followed Duncan. The end of the small canyon opened before him, the mountains giving way to a huge sweep of desert. The view was spectacular here, the river a small, shimmering snake winding through the vast plain of desert between the ranges of mountains on either side. He and Dizzy often stopped at the place to eat lunch when they were walking together.

"They're on the way," Duncan said as Nate approached and settled down in the small shade offered by a large boulder.

"Thanks."

Duncan reached in the pack and handed him a bottle of water. Nate poured more on Dizzy's face, wetting her hair, gently washing the dried blood off her forehead. Finally, she moaned. "Diz?"

"Nate?" Her voice was a whisper rasping against a too-dry throat.

"Drink," he said, propping her on his knee and holding the bottle to her mouth. She sipped. "A little more, come on." She sipped again.

Her eyes fluttered open, "Nate? What took you so long?"

"I was partying, Diz, what do you think?" He could hear the *thump, thump* of the helicopter as it approached.

"Thought so," she said, letting her eyes close again "What's that?"

"It's the chopper, here to take you back to town," Nate said, watching out of the corner of his eye as the pilot jockeyed the helicopter down in a level area at the end of the pass. One of the medics hopped out before they were all the way settled. He ran up the pass towards them.

"Captain Mondragon," he said, dropping down beside Dizzy and pulling items out of his kit.

"Hi, Ken," Nate said.

"What happened?"

"Her car was stolen, she's been out here for at least a couple of hours, maybe longer," Nate said. "I think she took a blow to the head, too, bullet maybe," he added, keeping his voice calm.

"Dr. Donovan, can you hear me?" Ken said, checking her pupils. "Do you remember me? We met at the dinner for the Institute? I came with Sal?"

"Yeah," she said.

"How do you feel?" he said, prepping her arm and starting an IV.

"Great."

"We're going to take you into town and get you checked out, okay?" He stood as they brought the stretcher up the pass. "You ready?" With Nate's help they lifted her gently onto the stretcher.

"Nate?" she said, her voice fading.

"Yeah, Diz?"

"My bag, in the first shelter."

"We found it, don't talk anymore, okay?"

"There's something in it, get Duncan, show it to him. I found it at the base of the trail up to the shelter, the one that heads into

Cholla Canyon Rock Shelter. Duncan will understand, get him, okay?"

"Yeah, I will. I'll be in to see you in a bit."

"Thank you, Nate." She opened her eyes and reached her hand out, he took it in his, giving it a gentle squeeze then put it gently back on the stretcher.

"You behave till I get there." He smiled at her, she smiled back and her eyes drifted closed.

Nate took his phone from Duncan and dialed the office. "Sal, rescue's bringing in Diz. She's in bad shape, I'm pretty sure someone attacked her. We're up at the pass, I'll be back in a couple of hours. I'll let you know what I find."

"Sure, Nate. Are you okay?" Sal asked, concern in her voice.

"Yeah," he said, harshly, then flipped the phone closed with a hard snap.

Nate stood beside Duncan as the helicopter lifted off, the sounds of the rotors echoing through the pass like rhythmic thunder. He watched it as the pilot made the long turn towards town and the hospital, the helicopter a tiny moving dot. Nate could see the white square marking the helipad from where he stood at the edge of the mountains.

"You okay?" Duncan asked from beside him.

"No, not really," Nate looked over at the archaeologist. "She wanted me to show you that statue. What's it mean?" He watched as the chopper began its descent towards the helipad.

"I'm not sure, where'd she find it?"

"Back in the pass, we should check it out on the way back, it might be why."

"Why? Why what?"

"She was attacked, Duncan, left to die out here, maybe that statue has something to do with it, I don't know." He turned towards Duncan. "But when I know..." He stopped himself.

"What?" Duncan said, picking up on the emotion in his voice.

"I'm not sure, but I might forget I'm a cop. Let me show you where she found that." He led the way back into the pass, pausing long enough to turn and see the chopper settle on the pad.

11

The heat was shimmering between the canyon walls as Nate and Duncan walked back into the mountains. It was quiet, even the insects silent in the height of the midday sun. Nothing was moving, even the shadows were static, held breathless by the heat. Nate paused at the base of the trail that led up to the rock shelter.

"This is the trail she was talking about," he said to Duncan.

The archaeologist squatted down, looking over the ground. "It's been disturbed here, probably where she pulled out the statue. Can't be sure though." He stood, brushing the dirt off his hands.

"I think we can be sure," Nate said as he opened Dizzy's bag and pulled out her camera. He turned it on, scrolling through the last few pictures. Then he handed the camera over to Duncan.

"Yes, this is where she found it," Duncan said, looking at the pictures. "But what's it doing out here?"

"That's probably the million-dollar question." Nate put the camera back in the bag. "Let's go up to the shelter, there is a pretty good view of the pass and the trail back into the mountains from there." He walked up the trail, noting the various footprints, both animal and human. The most recent he knew were Dizzy's, he recognized the distinctive tread of her sandals. He reached the top, automatically checking Duncan behind him and running his eyes quickly around the open area in front of him, making sure there were no threats present.

"A pretty good view?" Duncan said, stopping beside him. "This is amazing." He was looking off the edge of the cliff at the sweep of desert below. This side of the mountain plunged down hundreds of feet to the desert floor. "Hey, that's the edge of my dig, isn't it?"

Duncan pointed at a white spot just visible behind a bend in the mountain.

Nate peered over the edge. "Yeah, I think so. That must be the lab trailer. I hadn't thought about where you were in relation to the pass." He frowned as he noticed a plume of dust drifting up from the wash, a moment later a pick-up zoomed into view, heading up the utility service road. "Can you tell what's on the side of that truck?"

Duncan walked over and stood beside him shading his eyes. "Not really, a logo, but that's all. Where's he going?"

"Up the service road, heading towards the mountains. There's a bit of public land there between the developments. You sure you can't make out the logo?"

"Yeah, sorry."

"Hmm," Nate said.

"Hmm? What's hmm?"

"I don't know, a funny feeling all of a sudden. Don't know what, just hmm."

"Sure," Duncan said, walking into the shelter and looking at the petroglyphs on the walls. "Looks like some are missing."

"Every time we come up here more are gone," Nate replied. "Oh, damn, her favorite." He walked over to the empty spot on the wall. "A family of sheep, she loved that stupid thing, has dozens of pictures of it."

Duncan looked at him for a minute before stepping out of the shelter again. "This trail here, is this the one that leads out to the cave? I know how to get to it from where the dig is, but not from this side."

"That's it. It's not that easy from this side, it drops down, then goes up that face over there," Nate said, indicating the stark red-brown mountain across from them. "We have enough water for a bit. You want to wander down that way?"

"Sure," Duncan said, setting off down the trail.

Nate followed, listening to the lack of sound around him and watching the trail for any signs of movement. It had been well used lately, which was unusual. The trail seemed to dead end, and unless someone knew that the path continued around the mountain, they usually didn't venture very far down it. One set of footprints seemed to match the prints up in the shelter. He stopped, squatting down to get a better look at them. The prints turned off the main trail, following a faint game track that led down the mountain.

"Duncan? Let's go this way." He pointed down the trail. "Just for a mile or so, then we can head back." Nate led the way this time along the winding trail as it dropped between the huge pillars of the mountains. He stopped when he realized the path would take them down to the desert floor.

"This looks like it might drop down kind of where my dig is," Duncan said, looking over Nate's shoulder at the trail.

"I think it might." Nate started down the trail again. He had started to feel uneasy, for no reason that he could put a finger on, just a knot of tension between his shoulder blades. They had been walking for about half an hour when Nate decided it was time to turn around. They were in a fairly open area, but the trail was just about to narrow considerably, and he knew they needed to head back before their supply of water got too low. He stopped and pulled a bottle of water out of the pack. "Let's take a quick break here, then turn around, we can come back later, tomorrow maybe, with more equipment."

"Sounds good," Duncan said, taking a drink and scouting around as Nate squatted in the shade of a small oak.

Nate watched as Duncan wandered around, stooping to poke at something on the ground, then moving on. Nate chuckled to himself, he'd watched Dizzy do the same thing many times.. He always wondered what she saw, or didn't see, in the small rocks and other objects she picked up. She'd tried to explain more than once, patiently pointing out what she was looking at, but most of it didn't process. He'd told her one rock pretty much looked like another to him. She'd laughed and shaken her head. He was idly watching Duncan when the archaeologist stopped as if he'd hit a wall, staring down at the ground.

"Can you bring the camera over?" Duncan said, looking over at him.

"Coming." He got up and walked over to where Duncan was standing, staring at the ground. "What is it?"

"I think that's a gold bead. I thought we'd need a photo before I picked it up," Duncan said, taking the camera from Nate. He took seven pictures before he handed the camera back and bent to pick up the bead. "Egyptian, I think, Eighteenth Dynasty by the looks of it." He grinned. "I know, I'm supposed to focus on American archaeology, but Egyptology is still the crown jewel in so many ways, you know?"

Nate smiled back. "Yeah, Diz says something along those same lines, always apologetic, but still with excitement in her voice when she talks about it." He broke off and looked away for a moment.

"She'll be okay, Nate," Duncan said softly.

"Yeah," Nate cleared his throat and looked down at the bead Duncan was holding. "I'll be damned." He took it in his hand and turned it over. "I think this is like the one they found in Frank's stomach." He closed his eyes, concentrating on the photo he'd received. "I'm pretty sure of it." Nate dropped the bead into Dizzy's bag.

"So, what's a five-thousand-year-old bead from the other side of the world doing out here?" Duncan said, looking at Nate. "And for that matter, what the hell is another one doing in a murdered archaeologist's stomach?"

"Good questions," Nate said as he turned and walked back up the trail.

They stopped several times as they walked back to the car. Duncan was checking the various small sites that dotted the canyon. Each time they stopped, Nate went on the alert. He wasn't quite sure why, just that his instincts were on high alert. He backed up against a rock or cliff every time, keeping his back protected as he scanned the pass.

When they reached the mouth of the canyon, Nate went to look again at the place he was sure Dizzy had fallen. The dark spot of blood had dried to just a tiny stain on the red rock. Small pieces of broken stone scattered the area. Nate glanced up at the cliff face, a new scar on the stone, pink against the weathered rock. He turned and looked across the canyon, up to the ledge above them. Without thinking, he turned and walked up the steep trail to the ledge. Duncan followed him, the archaeologist's feet slipping on the gravel. A bright glint caught Nate's eye. He walked over to look at a small object on the ground.

"What is it?" Duncan was breathing heavily from the fast climb.

"Whoever was up here didn't pick up all his brass," Nate said, pointing down at the empty cartridge. "Sloppy." Nate froze when he heard the sound of a vehicle approaching, still a ways off, but definitely headed their way. He moved to where he could see up the road, then relaxed when he recognized the car. "One of mine," he said, looking at Duncan. "Sal must have sent them up here." By the time they got back to Nate's car, the other vehicle was parked.

"Cap?" one of the men said as he got out of the car.

"Hey, Ian, Andy, have you met Dr. Keogh?" Nate nodded towards Duncan. "There's brass up on the hill and I'll show you where someone took a shot at Dr. Donovan." He led the two men down to the mouth of the pass. He watched for several minutes before he was satisfied and turned back to Duncan, who was waiting at the car. "Time to head into town," he said, getting in the car.

As soon as he could get a signal, he called his office. Sal was on the phone before the first ring had completed. "Hey, Sal, thanks for rolling Ian and Andy."

"I called Manny, Nate, to let her know what was happening, she headed up to the hospital," Sal said. "She called a minute ago. Dizzy's okay, heat stroke, dehydrated, but okay. They are going to keep her overnight, I guess. But she's okay."

"Thanks," Nate said softly, surprised at the emotion in his voice. "I'll stop by there, then I need to come by the office."

"It's your day off, sit with Dizzy, Nate, come in tomorrow."

"You've been around her too much, Sal, stop arranging my life," he chuckled and snapped his phone closed, looking over at Duncan. "Diz'll be okay."

"That's good to hear, I was worried," Duncan replied. "She didn't look good when we found her."

"No, she didn't, for a minute I thought she was..." He couldn't finish the statement. "I know she has more lives than a cat, but sometimes I worry she might be running low. She does have a knack for coming out of things okay. Once when we were hiking she took a tumble down this long scree slope. I was sure she'd broken her neck, and when I get down to the bottom she's all scraped up and laughing hysterically. I nearly smacked her." He broke off, realizing he was babbling.

Duncan was looking at him, an intense look, he started to say something then stopped. "How long till we get into town?"

"About twenty minutes from here," Nate said, wondering what the archaeologist had intended to say. "If I go the speed limit."

"Which you're not."

"Which I'm not."

The hospital parking lot was crowded when they arrived. Nate casually parked in a "reserved" spot. "No one will tow my car."

"More perks of the job?"

"Yep," Nate said, getting out and heading into the hospital. He stopped by the information desk to get Dizzy's room number, then walked towards the elevators. Glancing in the windows of the gift shop as he walked past, he reversed direction and headed into the shop. Duncan followed him in. Nate picked up the small plush bighorn sheep that was displayed in the window and took it up to the counter, ignoring the look on Duncan's face as he did so. After paying for it he looked over at Duncan. "What?"

"Nothing."

The third floor was quiet. The air had a hushed quality that Nate always associated with hospitals, the sounds of conversation subdued, worry absorbing the noise. He nodded at the nurses sitting at their station as he recognized them.

Dizzy's room was in the far corner of the ward. Nate paused outside the partially closed door, listening to Manny's voice. She was chatting away, talking about something on the television. Nate listened for an answering voice, and when it didn't come his heart gave a funny skip. Duncan was standing behind him, waiting to go in. Nate finally pushed the door open.

Manny was sitting by the bed, she turned when they entered and smiled. "Hi, we were wondering when you'd get here," she said.

"Yeah, sorry it took so long, but we were looking around." Nate walked to the bed. "Hey, Diz. Look what I found." He set the sheep on the bedside tray.

She smiled, her cracked lips bleeding as she did. "Thanks."

"He was following me, so I figured he should be up here where you could keep an eye on him."

"You want to get a cup of coffee?" Duncan asked from behind him.

"Sure, there's an espresso stand downstairs," Manny said. "We'll bring something for you." She patted Nate gently on the back as she followed Duncan out of the room. He nodded and waited till he heard them leave before sitting down in the chair beside the bed.

"You look like hell," he said in a gentle, teasing voice.

"Thanks. I feel like hell," she replied, her voice still sounding raspy and dry.

"You scared the shit out of me, Diz."

"I was a little worried for a while too, Nate. I was beginning to think you wouldn't get there in time." She held out her hand. He took it. "Thanks, I owe you my life."

"Anytime. Of course, you do something like this again and as soon as you are up and around, I'll kill you myself."

"I'll remember that." She laughed softly. "Did you call Duncan about the statue?"

"He was with me, Diz."

"He was?" The confusion in her voice worried him. "How did I miss that?"

"It's okay, I think you have a pretty good excuse. I showed him the statue and we looked at where you found it, then wandered down the trail a bit. Looks like someone has been using the area a lot lately. We found something." He pulled the bead, now in a small Ziplock baggie, out of his pocket. "Looks like the one they found in Frank," he said, handing it to her. She took it and looked at it with a frown.

"Looks Egyptian."

"Yeah, that's what Duncan said when he looked at it," Nate said. "Diz? Are you up to telling me what happened?"

"Of course. Can I have some ice first?" She pointed to the cup on the tray. "Nice sheep, by the way. Oh, Nate, the family of sheep, it's gone." He saw tears sparkle at the edges of her eyes.

"I know, Diz. I saw, I'm so sorry."

"Thanks." Nate winced as she crunched on the ice, she grinned at him and took just a tiny bit more ice, crunching on it before she started. "I got back to the head of the pass and the car was gone. Someone took a shot at me, I think. And then when I was down, they shot the water pack. I heard them talking, two guys, one with a slight accent, East Coast I think, that funny flat A? They drove off and I headed to the other side to see if I could get a signal or make it to the highway, I didn't make it all the way." She stopped and looked over at him. "Thought I'd bought it, Nate."

He squeezed her hand, swallowing down the emotion that quiet admission caused in him. "Yeah, well, you didn't. We'll have to postpone dinner for a day or two."

"You could smuggle in some food, we could eat Thai right here."

"Only if the doctor says it's okay, Diz. You are going to behave even if I have to have them strap you in the bed, got it?"

"Yes, sir, captain, sir." She was grinning at him. He grinned back, the enormous sense of relief at knowing she was okay nearly undoing him.

Manny and Duncan returned a few minutes later. They brought a coffee for Nate and settled in the other chairs by the bed. Dizzy immediately started quizzing Duncan on the statue and the bead they had found. Nate listened as they discussed it, letting the words flow around him, some of them processing but most not as he mused on everything that had happened. Frank's murder and

Greg's near-fatal attack. A 5,000-year-old bead in Frank's stomach which was similar if not identical, to one they found in the mountains. Duncan's information that Frank was taking bribes. What did it mean? And why had someone taken a shot at Dizzy?

He focused back on the conversation. Dizzy had grown quiet and was listening to Duncan talking about some artifacts he'd seen on eBay. She had a frown on her face. Nate realized he was still holding her hand. Manny looked at him, smiling. He smiled back and raised his eyebrows, indicating he'd noticed how close she was sitting to Duncan. She blushed.

They'd been sitting with Dizzy for nearly three hours when a CNA came in with a large bouquet of lilies. Dizzy wrinkled her nose at the scent. Nate wondered who had sent them, Dizzy hadn't liked lilies since…He stood. "Where did those come from?"

"Aren't they beautiful? Mr. Scott had me bring them in," the girl said, turning them in her hands.

"Nate," Dizzy said warningly as he pulled his hand away from her. "Nate!"

He heard her but the words didn't register, he was out the door before he realized he was moving. Scott was standing by the nurses' station with a smug, indulgent smile on his face. "I was so worried when I heard," he was saying to the nurse behind the desk. "I've told her so many times to be careful in the mountains, that something could happen."

"Get out," Nate said, walking up to him.

"Ah, the savior, no doubt," Scott said, turning on him. "From what I've heard, you almost didn't make it in time," he said with a snide laugh. "And wouldn't that have been too bad? Poor little thing."

Nate wasn't sure exactly how it happened. One minute he was looking at Scott in his perfect suit and the next minute he had him up against a wall and Duncan was trying to pull him away. "Nate, come on, let him go."

Nate became aware of a uniformed security guard in the hallway, standing unsure of what to do. Nate dropped Scott, the other man nearly falling as the pressure was released. "Get out," Nate said again.

"You can't attack me like that, not in public." Scott's face was turning red.

"Anyone see anything?" Nate asked the crowd that had gathered around them. Silence greeted the question. Nate looked at Scott. "Get out."

Scott straightened his suit. "My lawyer will be calling you about this assault."

"Let him. And while you're at it, tell him if I see you in here again, I'll have you arrested for violating that protective order, got it?"

Scott turned and stalked out. Nate followed him as far as the elevators to make sure he left. When the doors slid closed, he realized his hands were shaking. He smiled at Duncan. "Thanks, killing him here might have been a bad idea."

"Nate? Want to tell me about it?" Duncan asked quietly. "It's more than just he tried to stop them hiring you, more than he's her ex, isn't it?"

"What?"

"It's more than that. Her reaction, your reaction, Manny said something the other night, then stopped herself. I know Scott and Dizzy lived together, she told me that, but what else?"

Nate looked at Duncan, debating with himself briefly, then walked over and sat down in one of the chairs in the small waiting room across from the elevators. He sighed. "It was about seven months ago. Yeah, she was living with the bastard. I never liked him."

"I bet," Duncan said.

"Yeah," Nate agreed. "But I tolerated it, you know. She's a friend, and she thought she was in love with him. I noticed things were off in her once or twice, and then a whole week went by, she avoided me the whole time. I finally called Manny, and she told me Diz had come to work that Monday with a black eye."

"Shit."

"I was pissed and called her. She said it was nothing, she'd taken a spill when she was out surveying, and she hadn't said anything because she was afraid I'd overreact."

"Which was the worst thing she could say."

"Pretty much. I didn't know what to do, you know. I was sure he'd hit her but couldn't do anything. Then…" He paused and ran a hand through his hair. "Then I really blew it."

"What happened?"

"I saw him at the town offices and told him if I heard that Dizzy had another black eye, I would be out to discuss it with him." He swallowed. "That night a call came in, I happened to be in my office and dispatch came and got me."

"Nate?" Duncan said.

"She was hurt. He'd beaten her pretty badly. I got there first. The neighbors had called, he was gone, and she was..." He stopped and swallowed. "It was probably a good thing he wasn't there. I stayed with her, you know, until she was safe in the hospital. They arrested him."

"What happened?"

"Diz. She wouldn't press charges. I tried everything and she refused. Damn stubborn... Sorry." He looked at Duncan, aware there were tears in his eyes. They came every time he remembered that night, arriving and finding her in the living room, beaten, frightened and so unlike the woman he'd grown to love. "Someday, Duncan, the bastard will make the right mistake and I'm going to take him down for it, and everything else. He likes to do this, taunting her, and there's something about him that just shakes her—she doesn't react like her usual self around him, never did."

"God, I'm sorry," Duncan said.

"Yeah, me too. Thanks," he said, standing. "We'd better get back."

The lilies were gone when they got back to the room. Dizzy looked at Nate, relief in her eyes. "You didn't kill him?"

"Not yet," Nate said.

"Too bad," she said, looking at him, her eyes sad, haunted for a minute.

"Diz?"

"So," she said, her voice falsely bright. "Didn't you say something about smuggling in some Thai food? Why don't you and Duncan go get some and bring back that picture of the bead in Frank's stomach you promised me, okay?"

"Diz, I don't think..."

"Please, Nate?"

"As long as the doctor says it's okay," Nate said. "You be a good girl till we get back."

"Thanks," she said, smiling at him. "I'll just take a nap. That'll keep me from misbehaving."

"Good idea." He gave her hand a squeeze. "Coming?" he asked Duncan. The archaeologist stood and they headed out to get food. They made a brief stop at ICU to check on Greg and see if Jack needed anything. Nate took an order for food from the cops standing guard before driving into town. As they left, he noticed Carter's huge vehicle pulling out of the lot. Nate followed it for several blocks before turning into the restaurant.

12

The hospital had grown quiet as the day faded, visitors were becoming less and less frequent. They were still sitting with Dizzy, and like the hospital she had grown quiet, too. Duncan noticed she was speaking less after dinner and had finally faded into silence. She was nearly asleep, quietly listening to the three of them talking.

"You need to go get some sleep," she said suddenly.

"We're okay, Diz," Nate said.

"No, you need to go, and I'm fine here. Just come back in the morning, okay?"

"Are you sure, Dizzy?" Manny said.

"I'm fine."

Nate stood and looked over at Duncan. "Okay, Diz, if you're sure. You need to sleep. I'll be back first thing." He gave her hand a squeeze and nodded at Duncan.

"Night, you two," she said.

"Be good," Nate said as he left the room. Duncan smiled at Manny and then followed Nate out into the hall. He was surprised to find the police captain talking to a uniformed officer. "No one in or out," Nate was saying as Duncan approached. "I'll be here in the morning when she gets released, but until then no one but the night nurses you've already cleared and the doctor."

"Got it, Cap," the cop said.

"Nate?" Duncan said, walking up to him.

"Just in case, Duncan. I don't think anything will happen here, but never hurts to be careful," he said as they walked to the elevators.

"Do you really think?"

"I'm not sure. All I know is Frank's dead, Greg is nearly dead, and Diz is here."

"She's going to be okay."

"I know, doesn't make what happened any easier," he said, getting into the car.

"I get it." Duncan was quiet as Nate drove through town. "You know, hmm," he said more to himself than to Nate.

"What?"

"I was thinking about those planes, Nate. Or maybe it was the same one? You and I saw one and then Dizzy and I saw one, but what if it was the same one?"

"What?" Nate said, looking over at him.

"And the day I shut down the dig, I was actually run off the road by a plane, it looked like he was trying to take off, or just had and was using the road."

"A plane nearly ran you off the road?"

"Yeah. I was pissed, but didn't connect it to anything, then, well, you know, it occurred to me, once or twice while I was out at the site we were buzzed by a plane. I didn't think anything of it at the time, but now it just seems odd, you know, always by us, not further out or down by the airstrip."

"Odd is right. But what does it mean?" Nate said, looking out the window with a frown on his face. "Whoever was in the plane we saw was heading north. Carter's land is out that way. And that truck, it was out by Carter's land as well."

"Uh, Nate?" Duncan said.

"Yeah?"

"That bribe I mentioned? To sign off without a survey?"

"Yeah?"

"It was Lisa Daniels."

"And Lisa means Carter." Nate tapped on the steering wheel wondering what it all meant. "But why? Hmm." He grinned. "Lisa?"

"Uh, yeah," Duncan said, hoping the blush didn't show. "She cornered me in the men's room at the Inn."

Nate laughed. "That must have been fun."

"Yeah, nearly as much fun as a third-degree burn."

"I bet it was," Nate said, grinning. "Lisa is always interesting."

"Oh yeah, really interesting."

"Would you be willing to call her? Tell her you're interested? Is there any way you could find out where the piece of land is?"

"Sure, I have to know the terrain to write up a quick report. They'll have to give me a topographic map to physically sign off on as well."

"Are you willing?" Nate said.

"Yes, of course."

"It could be nothing."

"You don't believe that, do you, Nate?"

"No, I don't, and knowing that, well." He shrugged.

"What is it?"

"It could be dangerous," Nate offered.

Duncan could hear the tension in his voice. "I know. But Nate, even if it has nothing to do with what happened to Frank Daniels, it is something."

"What do you mean?"

"They want me to sign off on land without a survey. Got to be a reason, even if it's just they know something is out there that might slow the development plans. So, it's something, even if it's nothing."

Nate laughed, shaking his head. "That bit of circular logic is almost as amazing as some I've heard come out of Diz's mouth."

"Should I take that as a compliment?" Duncan said.

"I'm not really sure." Nate pulled into Duncan's driveway. "Can I ask you a question?"

"What?"

"If they release Diz tomorrow, she'll probably want to go by the Institute which is fine, Manny can keep an eye on her and I can have a cruiser out front, but after that, well, uh."

"You're worried about her being alone at home?"

"Yeah, so, here's the question—should I ask her if she'd rather stay at Manny's or at my place? Or should I just tell her she's staying in my spare room, end of statement?"

"Does that work with her? The end of statement thing?"

"Hell, no. I'll give her the choice, and if she makes the wrong one, I accidentally ignore it, right?"

"Sounds like a plan," Duncan said, laughing. "I'll call you and let you know when and where I'm meeting Lisa."

"Thanks," Nate said as Duncan got out of the car. "Don't meet until you call me, okay?"

"I won't. I'll be down at the Institute around nine."

"I'll probably see you there, then. And hey, Duncan?"

"Yeah?"

"Thanks."

"Sure," he said, closing the Jeep's door. He waved as Nate pulled out and wandered towards his door. A squeak made him jump, he laughed as he saw a gecko race out of the shadows, out into the garden. He unlocked the door and kicked off his shoes. After a quick shower, he turned on the television, looking for something to watch for a minute or two. *The Mummy* with Boris Karloff was on the classic movie channel, and he settled down to watch.

Classical music woke Duncan. The music stopped and then started again. Duncan rolled over and looked at his cell phone. The music stopped again and a few seconds later started back up, the phone was sliding towards the edge of the nightstand, carried there by the vibrations that accompanied the ringtone. He reached out and managed to grab it before it slid off the table.

"What?" he answered, louder than he intended.

"Hey."

"Nate?" Duncan said, hoping he recognized the voice.

"You awake?"

"Nope." He sat up and looked at the clock.

"Want to get a cup of coffee before you head to the Institute?"

"Sure, I'll meet you in half an hour. I'll call Lisa while we're there."

"Part of the plan," Nate said. "See you there."

Duncan rolled out of bed and staggered into the shower. Ten minutes later he was feeling closer to human. He grabbed his laptop and notes and headed out the door, stopping for a minute as the heat hit him. Even after being there for months, he still wasn't used to that furnace blast in the morning. Duncan got in the car and turned the radio on. It was still quiet on the road, the few cars all heading further into town. The lot at the coffee shop was remarkably empty. Duncan parked next to Nate's Jeep.

Nate was sitting at his usual table, three cups sitting in front of him. "One's for you," he said as Duncan walked up to the table.

"Thanks," Duncan said, sitting down. "I think I've caught your coffee habit. My heart doesn't seem to work as well as it used to without coffee." He took a sip and looked over at Nate with raised eyebrows.

"I might have ordered you an extra shot or two by accident. They made it the way I order when I get a mocha," Nate said, shrugging. Duncan noticed dark circles under his friend's eyes.

"A mocha?"

"Don't tell Diz, I'll never live it down, but I get mochas now and then. Okay, six shot mochas, but mochas."

"The milk makes it more like food," Duncan pointed out helpfully.

"Right," Nate said. "How long did it take you to come up with that rationalization?"

"Not as long as you'd think," Duncan said, laughing. "You learn fast in grad school. The espresso bar by the science building even had these packets of 'coffee power' that had vitamins and, I think, added protein."

"And you lived on those for how long?"

"Months until I finished my thesis. Then I ate real food for a while, then back to power coffee for the doctorate."

"Fun. What the hell is that?" Nate asked when Bach started up.

"The Fugue in D Minor, BWV 565," Duncan said, pulling out his phone. He didn't recognize the number. "Hello?"

"It's Manny."

"Hey." He felt the stupid smile start on his face.

"Lisa Daniels called the Institute looking for you," she said, her voice clipped. Duncan groaned before he could stop himself, he heard Manny chuckle. "She wants you to call her about something. She wouldn't say what."

"Thanks, Manny. Are you in today? I was thinking I'd come by to do some research, but it's Sunday."

"Yes, it's Sunday, but I'm usually in for a bit. I thought if Dizzy was released, she'd want to come by."

"Okay, I'll be by in about an hour," Duncan said.

"I'll be here," Manny said. "See you then."

Duncan flipped the phone closed and looked up at Nate. "I forgot it was Sunday."

"I'm not sure what month it is, so forgetting the day is no worry," Nate said with a laugh.

"Lisa called looking for me. Let me make this call and get it over with." He pulled the slip of paper with her number on it out of his pocket and dialed. She answered on the second ring. "It's Duncan Keogh," he said.

"What can I do for you?" she purred.

"I wanted to talk with you about that survey. Can we meet?"

"Half an hour? The Inn?" she said.

"Sure, I'll be there." He broke the connection and looked at Nate. "Half an hour at the Inn."

"The Inn? Restaurant or a room?"

"What?" Duncan sputtered. "I hadn't thought of that. She must mean the restaurant, though, or she'd give me a room number, right?"

"Maybe," Nate said, grinning at him. "You might want to make sure you have pepper spray with you."

"Thanks."

Nate sighed and got up, coming back a few minutes later with more coffee. He sat down. "I need to head in and check on Diz in a minute."

"How is she?"

"When I called this morning, she was still sleeping, but her nurse said she'd be ready to go whenever I wanted to pick her up. I think Diz is a challenging patient. I already have a cruiser lined up for the Institute, so everything should go smoothly."

"Until you tell her she can't go home?"

"Yeah, until then. I might run out towards your site later, want to ride along?"

"Sure," Duncan said.

"Good." He grinned. "Assuming you survive Lisa, of course." He rose, picking up his coffee. "I'm off to the hospital, I'll see you at the Institute in about an hour."

"Yep," Duncan said, following him out of the shop. He dropped into his car and headed towards the Institute. The mayor's yellow Hummer passed him as he pulled onto the highway. Duncan watched it move through traffic before it turned up the street that led to the hospital.

The parking lot at the Inn was crowded, well-dressed people streaming into the building. Duncan finally found a spot and headed into the restaurant. There was a long line of people waiting to be seated. Duncan told the hostess he was meeting Lisa, and she pointed him towards the dining room.

Duncan realized most of the town council was scattered throughout the room. Bob Carter was sitting at a table with another man Duncan didn't recognize, Carey Scott was sitting in the corner by the door with Jacob Austin. Several of the developers he'd seen at the meeting were there as well. Lisa waved from a booth at the back of the room. Duncan groaned, the booth looked remarkably isolated.

Lisa patted the bench seat beside her. "I've been waiting, you're late."

"Yeah, sorry." Duncan looked around, wondering if he could grab a chair from one of the other tables without appearing too obvious about it. He shrugged and slid onto the seat. Lisa wiggled across the bench and slid her hand along his arm. Duncan looked at her, she had the dark mark of a bruise just below her collar. He tried to ease away, but she just scooted closer. He sighed. "Did you bring a map?"

"Of course." She reached under the table and picked up a map case, then opened it and pulled out a topographic map. "This is the area here." She ran a long, red nail down the map pointing to an area blocked off in yellow.

Duncan looked at the map. The area in yellow was out near his project site, branching off of the utility service road. He pulled the map closer, trying to get a better look at the piece of land. It looked like it ran along the edge of a strip of public land. "I'll need to drive out and look at it," Duncan said, looking up from the map.

"Can't you just sign off?" Lisa pouted.

"I need to look at it, to describe it for the report. If you want it done right, I need to write that report," Duncan snapped. She balked at his tone. "I'll go out tomorrow, take a picture or two and write your report. Does that work?"

"I...I'll have to talk to him, I think he just wanted you to handle it all without going out there."

"Sorry, if I put my name on it, I at least want it to look like I did it correctly. It's the best way to assure that no one else will go out there, you tell him that. I think I know what I'm doing." Duncan stood. "Call me and let me know."

"Don't you want to stay for a drink?"

"I have some work to do, thank you, another time." Duncan turned and walked away, feeling her eyes on his back, trying not to squirm as he left the dining room.

Matt Westfield stopped him as he walked towards the exit. "We still on for tomorrow?"

"Tomorrow?" Duncan looked at Westfield.

"The survey?"

"Oh, right. Can I move it to Tuesday?"

Westfield gave him a long appraising look. "Okay, Tuesday. Morning? Around eight?"

"Sure. It won't take long," Duncan said, forcing a smile.

"Thanks." Westfield walked towards his office. Price pounced out the door, grabbing Westfield and hauling him inside. Duncan made it to the exit and out of the Inn without anyone else stopping him.

Manny's car was parked at the Institute when Duncan arrived. A roadrunner zipped by as he walked up the path towards the building. He stopped to watch it for a minute as it wound its way through the rock and cactus garden beside the building. It reached the small fence on the far side and stopped, apparently forgetting it was a bird and could fly over the barrier. Duncan laughed as it ran back and forth before finally making a hop, assisted with wings, onto the top wire.

He shook his head and walked into the building. It was quiet, cool and dark. Manny hadn't turned the main lights on, and the entrance hall had the feeling of a cool evening, just at dusk. Duncan stopped by Manny's office, and she looked up with a smile.

"Good morning," she said.

"Hi." He stepped into the office. "I was wondering if I could use the empty office to get some writing done and maybe make a call or two?"

"Sure," she said, standing. She pulled a set of keys off the bookshelf. He followed her to the next office. She unlocked the door, and he walked in, setting his laptop on the desk. "Don't forget to dial nine for an outside line."

Duncan sat down at the desk and picked up the phone. An idea had started forming the night before and he wanted to follow up on it. A chance remark had perked to the top of his brain and wouldn't leave him alone.

"Hello?" Pat Kernan answered on the third ring. Duncan had met Kernan during the work on his dissertation. Trying to chase down some research, Duncan had called the anthropology department of a university in New Mexico, the department secretary had connected him to Kernan. They had quickly formed a friendship and regularly chatted.

"Pat? It's Duncan," he said.

"Duncan? Aren't you in Hell?"

"More than you can ever know," Duncan said with a chuckle. "I seem to remember you were thinking of taking a job out here a while ago."

"I was thinking about it, but the money wasn't worth it," Pat said.

"What do you mean?"

"I thought it was a simple survey, you know, didn't even require clearing, they actually wanted me to find things for them."

"And?" Duncan asked.

"Well, they wanted more," Pat said. "They offered good money, but they really wanted me to find something."

"Was it for the New Age inn? They make money on that kind of thing, giving tours and that kind of thing."

"Yeah, but Duncan, they wanted me to find something," Pat said. "Even if it wasn't there."

"What are you talking about?"

"They did have someone else working for them, but he got fired, I guess. I heard later he'd asked for more money. But he'd already started."

"Started what?" Duncan asked. "The survey?"

"That and..." Pat paused.

"Pat? What?"

"They wanted me to fabricate stuff, Duncan. The other guy had already started. He'd added a few petroglyphs to an arroyo wall. I couldn't, you know. The money was good, but my career is worth more than they were offering."

"They wanted you to fake finds?"

"Yeah, can you believe it? Most developers want you to not find anything, and those two want stuff found so bad they fake it. Nice, huh?"

"I can't believe it," Duncan said.

"And Duncan? When I was out there, before I turned down the job I found a piece of pottery in the arroyo."

"Brown ware?"

"Nope, Bell Beaker," Pat said.

"What?" Duncan scoffed in disbelief.

"Bell-Beaker. Honest-to-God Bell Beaker, as pure as if it'd come out of a barrow in Britain. I brought it back and showed it to Graham Winston. He said it's the real deal."

"In the middle of the Mojave in an arroyo with faked petroglyphs?"

"Yes, go figure, huh?" Pat laughed. "How's the dig going?"

"Didn't you hear?"

"Hear what? I just got back into town."

"We're shut down. Police investigation."

"What? Why?"

"We found a body, it's a local guy who went missing several months ago, cops think he was murdered."

"That's your dig? Damn, I read about it in the paper, that's rough. What are you doing with your time?"

"Taking advantage of the Baxter Institute to finish a paper," Duncan said.

"Baxter Institute? Shit, is that D.D. Donovan?"

"Yeah."

"Fun for you," Pat said. "I heard she's interesting to work with."

"Yep," Duncan said with a laugh. "Thanks for the info, Pat. See you at the conference in October?"

"Yeah, first round's on me," Pat said.

"It'd better be," Duncan said. He hung up the phone and looked at it thoughtfully. So, Westfield wanted artifacts no matter how they got there. Was Frank Daniels the archaeologist before they hired Pat? Price said something about blackmail yesterday. Could that have been Frank? And what was a Bell Beaker pot doing in a desert that also seemed to sprout Pre-Columbian statues and Egyptian beads? Duncan resolved to mention it all to Nate, then opened the laptop, hoping to get three pages finished before Nate and Dizzy arrived.

13

The hospital was quiet. The smells of breakfast—coffee, bacon and maple syrup—drifted through the hallway. It was dim in the room, the curtains closed against the bright light of the desert morning. Dizzy was flipping through the channels on the TV. The nurse had been in and pulled the IV, and Dizzy had been cleared to leave by the doctor. She was still tired, a headache was lurking behind her eyes and she still felt a little hot. When she'd asked about that, the doctor had assured her it was normal and would go away.

She got out of bed and padded over to the window, peeking out at the parking lot. An ambulance was pulling into emergency, a large family was piling out of a minivan, a bouquet of balloons in the man's hand. The woman was pushing a stroller. Bob Carter's SUV was parked in the second row. Dizzy turned towards the door for a minute, she'd thought she'd heard something in the hall. After a minute she went back to looking out the window, waiting for Nate's Jeep or Manny's Subaru to appear in the lot.

"Hello, Dym," Carey Scott said from behind her.

Dizzy froze. She turned around to face him, her heart was racing.

"Your friend Mondragon wouldn't let me see you yesterday," he said, stepping towards her.

"Leave, Carey," she said, trying to figure out if she could get to the nurse call button before he got close to her.

"I'm worried about you," he said gently. "You could have died out there, Dym."

"Get out," she said. Dizzy noticed the beads of sweat glistening on his forehead. "Go."

"But Dym, I've been thinking of you," he said. She made a move towards the bed. He got to her first and pushed her against the wall. She closed her eyes as he put his hand on her face.

"Get out," she whispered. Her heart was beating against her ribcage, and she knew her breathing was near to hyperventilation. "Just get out, please."

"Not yet, Dym," he said. "We need to talk about us."

"Please." She felt tears pricking at her eyes. He was close, bending closer. She turned her face as far away as she could. "Don't touch me, go, please, please, go."

"Let go of her," a soft voice said from the door. It was barely audible, but Dizzy heard it clearly. "Leave."

Scott let her go and turned towards Nate. "Mondragon. Good to see you."

"Get out," Nate said, walking towards them. "Get out or I'll shoot you," he said with a friendly smile.

"What did you say?" Scott asked.

"You heard me, no witnesses this time, Scott," Nate said. "If you're lucky, you'll just get off with an arrest."

"Nate," Dizzy said desperately. "No."

He looked at her for several long moments. "You have three seconds to get out, Scott."

"Or else what?" Scott laughed. "She won't press charges, even with the restraining order."

"I guess we're back to shooting then."

Scott took a step towards Nate. "You wouldn't."

"Want to bet your life on it?" Nate said, his voice was still soft, almost gentle.

"Cap?"

"Kevin?" Nate said to the cop in the door without turning away from Scott.

"Doc wants to talk to you about Greg," he said, stepping into the room. "Everything okay?"

"Yeah, Mr. Scott was just leaving, can you make sure he does?"

"Sure," Kevin said. "Mayor wants to talk to you, too." The big cop waited by the door until Scott walked out of the room.

Dizzy watched him leave before turning to Nate. "Thanks."

"You should have let me arrest him," Nate said. "Or at least shoot him."

"No," she said quietly. "Please, Nate, let it go."

"Diz," he said then stopped and took a deep breath. She could tell he was trying to change the subject. "Ready to go?"

"Been ready for hours," she said, walking out of the room. The doctor was waiting in ICU when they stopped to check on Greg.

"I'm sorry, Captain, we don't know how it happened." The doctor was frowning. "But he's still alive."

"Do you know what happened?" Nate snapped.

"Someone screwed up the meds. I hate to say it, but it happens sometimes. He'll pull through, though," the doctor said.

Dizzy was watching Nate's face while he spoke with the doctor. She saw Bob Carter standing in the waiting area outside the doors to the ICU. Dizzy saw Nate's eyes slide away from the doctor to the mayor and then back again. He was frowning.

"Thanks, doc," Nate was saying to the doctor. Dizzy watched Carter as he stopped a woman in scrubs and spoke with her, his big friendly smile painted on his face. The woman said something with a gesture towards Nate, and Carter looked up. Dizzy saw something cross his face as he looked at Nate, she couldn't put a finger on it, but it worried her. "Just one more minute, Diz," Nate said, touching her arm to get her attention.

"Okay," she replied. He walked over to the officer who had come into the room, Kevin Jones. The name came to Dizzy with an image of the big man and his tiny wife dancing at the Institute's anniversary party a few months before.

"Want to tell me how Scott got into that room?"

"I only stepped away for an instant, Cap. There was a disturbance down the hall and I..." Kevin's shoulders slumped. "No excuse, Cap. I'm sorry."

Nate took a deep breath and let it out slowly. "Don't ever let it happen again."

"No, sir," Kevin said, a look of profound relief on his face. "Never."

"Stay down here. No distractions."

"No, sir."

Nate turned back to Dizzy. "All settled," he said. "Are you okay? Do you need a wheelchair?" He looked so concerned that she started to laugh. He grinned at her.

"I think I can walk." She tucked her hand through his arm. "Can I go to work for a while, Nate? I don't really want to hang around home by myself, and I have a ton and a half of paperwork that has to be done. Manny and I can't stay on top of it anymore, what with everything else I have to do." She got the words out in a rush, hoping to forestall a protest.

"If you promise to be a good girl," Nate said as they stepped out of the building. The heat hit her hard and she swayed. Nate shifted his arm, putting it around her waist to offer some support as he guided her to his car. He helped her in and hopped in the driver's seat. "You can spend the day in the office. The office, Diz, and you are to not overdo it or anything, no going out, just office work."

"But, Nate," she said, teasing.

He turned on her. "God damn it, Diz, no." His face was red, and his eyes were angry. "You stay in the office. If you go out, I swear I'll tie you in your chair...I'll..." Nate looked at her for a minute, she saw the sudden anger drain out of his eyes, replaced by worry and concern. "Please, Diz, just for today?"

"I'm sorry." She put her hand on his arm. "I was teasing. I don't want to be out in the heat at all."

He patted her hand before turning the car on. "I'm not ready for teasing about it, yet."

"Sorry," she said again. "Do you like the archaeologist?"

"What?" Nate said, looking over at her.

"Do you like him?"

"I love that."

"What?"

"The way you can come out of left field with something and just expect everyone to be out there with you."

"What do you mean?" she asked, she could see a small smile playing on his lips.

"You can be utterly random sometimes. I'm sure it makes perfect sense in that mess you call a brain, but for the rest of us, well, it can be confusing."

"Nate!" She wasn't sure if she should laugh or be offended.

"Once it happened, I'll never forget." He was still smiling, lost in the memory. Dizzy watched his face as it softened. "We were out with Manny and that guy she dated for a while, and we were talking about movies when all of a sudden you pipe up with 'I wonder if a Tasmanian Devil has the jaw strength to bite through a mammoth leg?' I remember the guy gave me the funniest look because we were talking about that new comedy about vampires."

"Oh, yeah, I think I was thinking about..."

"Diz?"

"Nate?"

"I'm driving, don't try and explain your logic, I'll wreck the car trying to follow it," he said, laughing at her. "Why were you asking about Duncan?"

"No reason, just an idea."

"You'll be nice to him, won't you?" Nate glanced over at her.

"I'm always nice.".

"Yeah, nice. I saw you make that poor historian cry that night."

"He was an idiot."

"He was an expert in his field, or so the pamphlet said."

"An idiot expert, then." She was watching his face as they spoke. She could see something was weighing on him. "What's up?"

"How do you do that?"

"Do what?"

"Get in my head like that."

"My Dizzy sense is tingling," she said gently. "What is it?"

"Duncan...Frank..." He sighed. "Did you know Frank was clearing land for developers?"

"Yeah, he talked about it. Why?"

"Did he ever..." Nate stopped.

"Shit," Dizzy said.

He looked over at her. "What?"

"He was taking bribes, wasn't he?" She was suddenly angry. "He was, wasn't he? Nate? Was Frank taking bribes?"

"Someone kind of implied to Duncan he was," Nate said. "Are you okay?" He turned into the parking lot at the Institute.

"Dammit, Nate. I told him it was a bad idea. I told him flat-out it was wrong. He mentioned something in passing once. I thought he'd decided..." She sighed. "I knew. I've known since he freaked one day when I offered to help with a survey. I just didn't want to admit it to myself. Dammit."

"Sorry," he said, getting out and walking around the car to give her a hand.

"Is it why he's dead?" she demanded as they walked to the door and into the cool building. She sighed as they entered, letting the cool air flow over her. Nate paused for a minute in the door. He glanced out at the parking lot, a frown on his face before he looked back at her.

"I don't know, it's an idea, but there's that gold bead and some other tidbits that have come to light."

"Trying to string me along?" She laughed as they headed into the building. Manny popped out of her office as they approached, and Duncan appeared in the office next door. Dizzy smiled at her assistant and took a long look at Duncan. "Hi, guys."

"You need to go back and sit down, Dizzy. I'll bring you something cold out of the fridge, okay?" Manny said.

"I'm okay, a cold drink would be appreciated, though."

"I'm heading to the office and see if I can get some work done," Nate said. "Then I'll be back. No leaving, Diz, till I get back, okay?"

"Yes, sir! I'll behave."

"Good girl." He stepped aside as Manny came into the office with a can of soda. "I'll be back in a couple of hours to check on you." He waved at Manny and walked out. Dizzy heard him speak with Duncan for a moment.

"Do you like Duncan?" Dizzy said to her assistant. She laughed when Manny blushed. "Okay, got it. Would you ask him to come to my office when he has a minute?" Dizzy said. Manny nodded and walked out. She settled back in her chair and opened her computer, she was still waiting for it to boot up when Duncan stuck his head in the door.

"Manny said you wanted to speak with me?" he said, stepping into the office.

"Yeah, thanks. I've been thinking."

"Yes?"

"Do you like teaching?"

"What do you mean?" he asked, leaning against the bookcase. "I like it well enough, I guess."

"Do you plan on staying in academia?"

"I hadn't really thought about it all that much. I was offered the teaching position right as I finished the doctorate, it seemed like a good idea at the time."

"Would you consider doing something else?"

"You mean something like play archaeologist without dealing with students, professors and 'publish or perish'?" His voice sounded wistful.

"Something like that," she said. "I'm buried here. I've been thinking of adding another staff member here at the Institute. I was wondering...Would you consider staying here?"

"Here?" Duncan looked surprised. "In Hades Wells?"

"Yeah, here in Hell," she said, smiling at him. "Maybe at the Institute?"

He looked at her. "Are you serious?"

"Yeah, I am. I can offer a pretty competitive wage. Think on it?"

"Okay! I will." He glanced at her desk. "Can I help with anything?"

"Not right now, but maybe, just maybe, I can get through a tiny pile of this paperwork before something else really fun happens."

"Fun?"

"Yes, my life is never-ending fun," she said, shoving a pile off onto the floor.

"What are you doing?"

"The important ones always land on top, that's where I start," she said.

"Sometimes being around you gives me a headache."

"Are you a little bit nauseous too?" She was grinning at him.

"Maybe," he said, smiling.

"Oh good, I was beginning to think I'd lost my touch." She bent over to pick up the papers on the top of the pile. "Back to work."

The phone had been ringing and Dizzy was ignoring it, waiting for Manny to answer. She'd been back in the office for about an hour when the intercom beeped.

"What is it?" she said.

"Leslie Clark is on the phone," Manny answered.

"Line one? Thanks," Dizzy said picking up the phone. Leslie Clark ran a museum and research library in southern California. "Les, what can I do for you?"

"Hey, Dizzy, how's life in Hell?"

"Warm," she said, laughing.

"I bet, the one time I was there I felt slow roasted," Clark said, Dizzy could hear the smile in his voice. "I heard Duncan Keogh was heading up the Powell U dig out there this summer."

"Yeah, I heard that too."

"How'd he end up in Hell? Mouth off to Martin?" Clark was laughing.

"Something like that, I'm sure."

"I read that article of his on the lithic culture of the Lower Bajada, good stuff."

"You done with the small talk, Les?" Dizzy said, knowing that if she didn't distract him, they would be discussing Paleolithic cave art or indigenous pottery and never get to the reason for his call.

"Oh yeah, sorry. Something came up on one of the auction sites today, I was checking, you know, to see if anything important was there. There were thefts of Mayan goods about a month ago right out of an excavation. Anyway, I found something, looked like something from the valley, thought I'd call. I just emailed the link. The seller is in Arizona somewhere, in fact it looks like several items I'm pretty sure were stolen have a shipping address out of Arizona."

"Isn't the internet lovely? Stolen goods marketed right out in public. Makes me sick," she said, opening the email from him and clicking on the link. Her heart skipped a beat when she saw what it was. "My sheep! Thanks, Les, you're right, they came from here."

"Thought they might have," he said. "Good hunting, Dizzy."

"Talk to you soon, Les." She hung up the phone and dialed Nate's cell.

"Are you still being good?" he asked as he answered.

"Good as gold," she said. "I just got a call from Les Clark."

"Diz? What is it?"

"My sheep, Nate. They're up on an auction site, shipping from Arizona. I looked around and there are several other items I'm sure are from around here," she said, scrolling through the seller's items. "Oh, my God."

"What is it?" Nate said.

"Hang on," Dizzy said. "Duncan!" she yelled. The archaeologist came barreling out of his office and into hers.

"What?"

"Look." She turned the laptop towards him.

"Sonofabitch!" He was staring at the screen.

"What?" Nate demanded.

"Is that?" Dizzy said to Duncan.

"Yeah, I'm pretty sure it is," he said, looking at her.

"Diz!" Nate yelled.

"Sorry, Nate," Dizzy said. "The sandal from Duncan's dig, it's up on the site as well."

"Is he sure?"

"He looks pretty damn sure, you should see him, Nate."

"I'll be there in twenty minutes," Nate said.

"Okay, we'll see you then. Drive safe," she said with a wink at Duncan. "He'll be here in a minute." She hung up the phone and sighed. "That offer to help? Want to give me a hand tracking this guy?"

"Let me grab my computer," Duncan said, turning to the door.

"Grab Manny too."

"What?" Duncan turned back, a blush coloring his cheeks.

"Bring her back with you," Dizzy laughed.

"Right."

Dizzy watched him walk down the short hallway before turning to the computer again, scrolling through the various items for sale. Not only were there more pieces from the Southwest, some Mayan, a jade piece mostly likely Chinese, figurines, one of which she knew had been in a museum in the Iraq and three gold Celtic pieces—including a torc. All of them shipping from Arizona.

She stared at the wall. Maybe this was why Frank was dead.

14

The Sunday morning churchgoers were already off the road as Nate left the Institute and headed in towards his office. He was worried about leaving Dizzy with just Manny and Duncan to keep her from running amok. He knew she generally got her way with Manny, and he suspected Duncan wouldn't be able to stand up to her wheedling and whining.

It was quiet in the building when Nate arrived, he was one of the only people in the offices. They only kept a skeleton crew in on Sundays—just the dispatcher and the desk sergeant, most of the other desks were empty. The other cops rotated shifts, but for the most part it was quiet on Sundays, even the ever-vigilant Sal took the day off.

Sal must have worked late the night before, there were several orderly piles of files on his desk. After staring at them in disgust for a moment, he walked out of his office to the coffeepot and punched the on button. Sal always left it ready for emergencies, and he had a feeling today was going to be one of those days.

He was on his third cup and halfway through a report on a missing hiker when he sensed someone. He looked up, Lisa Daniels was standing in the doorway of his office. "Can I help you?"

She stepped into the room and closed the door behind her. "I need to talk to you," she said in a breathy near-whisper.

"About what?"

She leaned against the door, and he could smell her perfume, it was wafting over towards him, a heady fragrance. She walked over to the desk, and stopped beside it, not quite coming around. "It's well, I think I need your help," she said.

"What is it?".

"It's Bob, I'm frightened of him," she said. "He's gotten involved in something bad." She emphasized "bad" with the same gravity as a three-year-old reporting on the misbehavior of a sibling.

"Bad?" Nate asked.

"Yes, it's how he gets his money, you know." She sighed. "And then, the other night after I told him he needed to stop, well, he did this," she said, tugging on collar of her shirt to expose several black and blue marks on her neck.

"Would you like to make a report?" he said

"No, I want your help to make him stop."

"I need you to make a complaint before I can arrest him."

"Please, Nate, I need your help." Something in her face changed for a minute. "He could really hurt me next time. He gets off on it."

"Carter?" Nate shook his head. "What's going on, Lisa?" he asked gently.

"Do you ever wonder about the things you've done?" she replied sadly.

"Let me help," he said gently, responding to the near despair he saw in her eyes.

"There's nothing left, Nate. No help." She reached out and took his hand and met his eyes, for a moment he saw them reflect fear and sadness, then it was gone. "See you around." She turned and left. Nate stared at the closed door, wondering what that had been about, and promised himself he'd follow up on it.

Nate finished the report on the missing hiker. The man had disappeared into the mountains three days ago. Search and Rescue had failed to find any trace of him, and they were pretty sure he'd stumbled into one of the many open mines in the mountains. Nate picked up another piece off the stack of papers. A small-time drug dealer had been busted and had hinted that he had information that could be valuable, if the cops were willing to bargain. According to the report, he was willing to give them information on a major drug supplier in the valley in return for no jail time and, as he put it, "safe passage" out of the valley.

Nate looked thoughtfully at the report. Drugs had always been a problem, at least as long as he'd been with the department. The surrounding desert was pretty much empty, and the river served as a great navigation aid for people flying in and out. They typically used small planes that could land in the desert and be gone before the pick-up was even there. He walked out of his office towards the front of the building, stopping in front of the huge map on the wall. He examined it for a long time before walking back to his office.

As he headed back through the department, he glanced out the windows and into the courtyard of the town offices. Nancy, the police dispatcher, was out on her break, puffing away at one of the obnoxious cigars she had recently taken to smoking. She was chatting with a cop in uniform, Nate recognized Roy Norton, a recent addition to the department.

Nate was turning away when furtive movement in the area shaded by several leafy acacias caught his eye. Lisa had found someone else. She was pressed against the wall as he kissed her. Nate froze when he realized who it was that Lisa was grinding against. Carey Scott. He wandered to his office, the scene in the courtyard still distracting him. Nate dropped down behind his desk. A moment later the phone started ringing. It was Dizzy.

Nate was on the road towards the Institute five minutes later. He wondered what else from the trailer was for sale. They would bring him up to date when he got there. The problem was how to head out into the desert without Dizzy trying to come along. Nate pulled into the lot at the Institute and got out of the Jeep. Dizzy was waiting by the door and nearly pounced on him when he walked in.

"We found more," she said excitedly. "Duncan recognized the pot and the two bifaces from the trailer as well. The seller also has..." she paused dramatically.

"Waiting for the music, Diz?"

"I keep hoping, you know.".

"Pretend the music played," he said, smiling at her.

"Okay, he has a small string of..."

"Gold beads? Maybe Eighteenth Dynasty Egyptian?"

"Yes!" she said, her eyes sparkling. "It's a small string and not identical to the one you had but damn close, probably from the same individual if not the same necklace."

"Good work," he said as they walked back towards her office. Manny and Duncan were sitting at Dizzy's desk, a laptop opened in front of them. Nate recognized it as Duncan's. "You're all in on it?"

"Yeah," Duncan said, looking up at him.

"I need to run back out towards your site." Nate did his best to sound casual so Dizzy wouldn't try and weasel her way into coming along.

"Oh, can I go?" Duncan answered in the same tone.

"You two think you're sly, right?" Dizzy said with a grin.

"What do you mean?" Nate said.

"All casual, but don't worry. I'm not really up to it, and I want to chase this guy down through a few more auction sites. I'm hoping I can find one with a little more info."

"Nice thought, isn't it?" Duncan said.

"He might make a mistake. You never know."

"Okay, we'll be back in a couple of hours," Nate said. "There's a cruiser out front, Diz, and if you need help just holler."

"Holler?" she said, laughing. "Okay, Nate, if anything comes up, I'll holler."

"Good girl," he said, laughing with her. "Let's go."

They stopped by the office Duncan had been using long enough for him to grab the keys to the trailer in case they needed in, and then they walked out to the Jeep. Nate glanced around the parking lot to make sure the police vehicle was clearly visible from the highway, hoping it was enough to warn anyone off.

It was quiet as Nate maneuvered through traffic heading out of town. He couldn't quiet the nagging voice that there was something out there, something important. It had been getting louder the last day or two, and now it was nagging at him in a continual stream.

"Dizzy offered me a job," Duncan said suddenly.

"What?" Nate glanced over. "Really?"

"Yeah, she said that she has been thinking of adding another staff member and then asked if I would consider staying here."

"And?" Nate asked.

"I have a good position at the university, you know, not many people my age have adjunct professorships."

"But?" Nate said. "I hear a really big but in there."

Duncan looked over at him. "I thought it's what I wanted, you know, the professor life, but it's a bigger pain in the ass than I ever dreamed it would be. My students mostly hate me because I am pretty close to their age, Jeremy Martin dislikes me because I challenge him, my colleagues treat me like a student, and I hate the publish or perish thing. I either have to research or teach, and so both suffer." He took a deep breath. "Sorry, don't mean to bitch."

"I did ask, I think." Nate pulled onto the wash road and headed into the desert. "Do you think you'll take the job?"

"I'm not sure, I'm going to think about it a bit and maybe talk to Dizzy about it again," Duncan said.

"Sounds good."

"Where exactly are we going?" Duncan asked as Nate zoomed up the road and on to the desert floor.

"Your dig first, and I want to walk a ways in the direction of those tracks, then I don't know, we'll see from there," Nate said.

"What are you looking for?"

"Honestly?" Nate laughed. "I have no idea I'm hoping to just start poking under bushes and see what jumps out."

"Smart," Duncan agreed. "As long as it's not a poisonous snake that pops out."

"Yeah, problem is, though, Duncan, I'm pretty sure that's what's out there," Nate said grimly. "Whoever this is pretty damn poisonous."

"Right," Duncan said.

Nate pulled up beside the cruiser parked at the site. He waved to the man standing watch by the trailer as he got out of the car. "Hi, Johnny," he called as he and Duncan walked onto the site.

"Captain," the cop on duty, Johnny Bauman, answered.

"How's it been?"

"Mostly quiet, Cap. There was a car out on the power-line road early this morning, it was still dark, right after we came on shift. We were early," he said with a shrug. "He was heading back into town, whoever he was, moving pretty fast."

Nate glanced over to where he knew the power-line road ran, just to the north of where they were standing. "Thanks, Johnny, keep your eyes peeled."

"Always!"

Nate walked along the edge of the trailer and then out towards where the large hole marked the removal of the core. He looked down at the tracks the vehicle had left, then squatted down to get a better look. He stood and walked along the path the tracks had made, the drag mark from the core clearly visible as well. Nate glanced at Duncan, the archaeologist looked sick. They walked on, the drag mark ended but the tracks continued across the desert. Nate followed them, head down, focused on the ground.

"Nate?"

Nate looked up, Duncan had drifted to the east, moving closer to the edge of the mountains. "See something?" he asked, walking over.

"I think, well, this is what you do, but I think someone has been going this way," he said, pointing along a narrow track leading to a break in the rock wall of the mountains.

Nate looked along the line Duncan indicated and then followed behind the archaeologist as they headed to the cliff face. Nate stood looking up at the mountain, trying to gauge where they were in relation to the dig and town. Duncan was standing in front of the break, a large vertical crack in the wall. He put his hand in and looked back at Nate with a grin. "It might be kind of tight, but..." and he slipped into the mountain.

"Duncan?" Nate stepped to where the archaeologist had disappeared. He peeked into the crack, looking back down the track to the road. In the slightly different light, he could see the track of a car clearly, whoever it was had been there many times, the faint ruts leading to an area of packed earth, obviously where they had been parking.

"Nate?" Duncan's voice drifted out of the crack in the rock wall.

"Coming," Nate said, squeezing into the opening. It was a tight fit. He glanced up, he could see a small sliver of blue sky far above him. A tiny spark of fear flared, the feeling of being trapped and unable to escape, not quite full-blown claustrophobia, but something very close to it.

He pushed through and stepped out the other side, trying to look collected. Nate ran a hand over his face. It was hotter here. The seam had opened up into a small box canyon, the mountains soaring overhead. A game trail ran up the eastern wall. Duncan was pacing along the edge of the rock wall to Nate's right.

"I'm going to go up the trail for a sec," Nate said, pointing at the steep track that led out of the canyon.

"Okay, I'm going to poke around over here," Duncan said.

"Everything okay?"

"What?" Duncan looked up. "Yeah, fine, just hunting."

Nate started up the trail, the stones rolling out from under his feet as he went up, once or twice using his hands as well to steady himself. He reached a small plateau and stood, looking back down at the trail he had ascended. He was at least a hundred feet above the canyon floor, the track back down looked like it dropped off the edge of a cliff.

Nate turned and walked further up the trail. It was not quite as steep here. The track wound around a large boulder, the face of the rock partially covered with petroglyphs. He smiled, thinking of bringing Dizzy out to show her the stone. Nate glanced ahead of him and stopped. It suddenly looked familiar. Looking in the direction he'd come, he could see Duncan was still wandering around far below him.

In front of him, the track split, one trail leading deeper into the mountains, the other running along the edge of the cliffs. Nate now knew it would lead to the small clearing where he and Duncan found the gold bead and then over to the pass where the petroglyphs were taken and where someone tried to kill Dizzy.

He stood looking over the cliff at the valley. Below him was the strip of public land between Coyote Estates and Golden Arroyo Homes. Nate noticed the long, faint track that looked almost like a road, running north to south on the desert below him—perfect for a landing strip, and there was a wash that connected to it. He'd long suspected the mayor was involved in the local drug trade. This seemed like proof.

Nate turned back to the path, slowly walking back towards the canyon, scouting along the path. Something off the edge of the trail, under a large cholla, caught his eye. He reached under the cactus and carefully fished out the object. A hiking boot, size eleven. Nate turned it over in his hand, the tread on the bottom matched one set of prints heading down the trail from the opposite direction of the canyon. Someone had walked over the trail from the pass. Dried blood was splattered on the toe of the boot. It could be the missing hiker, but what was his boot doing here?

"Nate?" Duncan's shout broke into his musing.

"Yeah?"

"You might want to get back down here," Duncan said, something in his tone alerted Nate.

"Be right there." Nate jogged along the path and then slid down the steep trail. When he reached the bottom, he noticed Duncan sitting on the ground at the back of the canyon. "Are you okay?"

"No."

Nate stopped beside the archaeologist, running his eyes over him looking for an injury. Duncan's face was white, he looked almost like he had been struck. "What?" Nate asked.

Duncan shifted so Nate could see the hole in the cliff wall. Duncan had moved a stone from in front it, to Nate it looked like the opening of an old mine. He bent down so he could see in. "Holy shit!" He dropped down on the ground beside Duncan.

"That doesn't even begin to cover it," Duncan said looking at him, then back at the small mine and the glittering objects inside. "I haven't touched anything, but I can see Egyptian, Mayan and at least one piece of Near Eastern art I know was taken from a museum."

Nate was shaking his head. "How much is this worth?"

"Millions," Duncan said. "I found that too." He pointed to a bag full of white powder.

"We found that shit over by where Greg was attacked," Nate said thoughtfully. "Our guy might use as well as import the stuff." He couldn't take his eyes off the golden objects glinting in the sun. "I guess that explains this." Nate held the boot out. "Missing hiker, must have stumbled on whoever owns this stuff."

"What do we do?"

"Put the stone back, let's see who comes after this," Nate said, standing. "I'll let my guys at your site know to keep an eye on it, maybe he'll come and get it sooner rather than later."

Duncan rolled the stone back into place and stood. They were silent, each lost in their own thoughts as they walked towards the opening. As he waited for Duncan to squeeze through, Nate noticed something caught under the edge of a jagged rock. He pulled it out. A small survey compass, the string broken, engraved "Frank Daniels." Nate dropped it in his pocket and followed Duncan back into the desert.

15

The heat was shimmering off the desert floor as they walked back towards Duncan's dig. Nate saw several turkey vultures circling overhead, drifting on the thermals, hoping to find a meal. The mirage was flowing over the ground like water, distorting everything around them.

"What's it doing out here?" Nate said, more to himself than out loud.

"It'd be a good place to keep it," Duncan said. "You'd have to know that canyon was there."

"I found Frank's compass back there. He must have found the place."

"Why didn't he say anything? He had to know what that stuff was."

"Maybe he did say something, only to the wrong person." Nate frowned. They stopped beside the large cooler sitting in the shade of the trailer. Nate pulled out a bottle of water for each of them.

"You mean it's why he's dead?"

"It's what I'm thinking," Nate said, walking to his Jeep. Bauman was talking with his partner as they approached. "Johnny, Tony, keep an eye on that road over to the north, okay? Don't go over or anything, just give me a call if anyone heads out this way."

"Sure, Cap," Bauman said, his partner nodded.

"Thanks," Nate said. He got into the Jeep and turned it on, letting it idle for a minute as Duncan settled into the passenger seat. He took one last look across the site. Bauman had his cell phone out, calling someone. Nate let his eyes drift north, along the road and out towards the developer's lands. "It explains where the money is coming from," Nate said. He was surprised when he heard his voice.

"What?"

"Sorry, I was thinking out loud, but drugs and maybe the other stuff would explain where his money is coming from," Nate said.

"Who?"

"Bob Carter. This is pretty close to his land, and I think you're right about the planes. He came into money, rather suddenly, about nine months ago. He said it was investors, but if he were running drugs, it would explain the money."

"Yeah, and Lisa's involvement," Duncan said, musing. He looked over at Nate and noticed something in his friend's eyes. "What?"

"Lisa, she paid me a visit earlier," Nate said uncomfortably.

"Fun?"

"Oh yeah, the most fun I could have and not shoot myself." He took a breath. "Actually, something was off. I think she might be into something bad."

"She say who?"

"Carter, but..." Nate stopped himself, not even sure where the thought was going.

"Anyone else?" Duncan said quietly.

"What?"

"Who've come into money?"

"Well, Matt Westfield had a windfall, never explained it. No one else suddenly better off," Nate said, thinking.

"You sure?"

"What are you driving at?"

"I don't know, the cop thing is your job."

"Okay, Dan Hill showed up and started purchasing land about eighteen months ago, then there was, no, he left town already. Carey Scott sold some land a few months back for quite a chunk, or so Diz said. It's when he bought that Mercedes. Then let's see, one of the council members managed to get investors for some stupid project; the project fell through, but the money stayed."

"So, actually lots of people," Duncan said with a grimace.

"Yeah, but only one of them that owns property out here and is with Lisa Daniels," Nate said definitely.

"Uh huh," Duncan said quietly. Nate looked over, the archaeologist was staring out the window.

"What is it?"

"Huh? Nothing, just thinking," Duncan looked over at him. "I might need more coffee," he said with a grin. "Let's stop on the way back. I'll buy. I think my heart is stopping."

Nate laughed. "Mine stopped about an hour ago, I just didn't want to say anything that might freak you out."

"Well, a dead man driving is worrying."

"Not dead, not yet, but it's going to be close," Nate said, grinning.

Nate pulled up at the Institute and got out, carefully balancing his coffee and the frozen coffee he'd purchased for Dizzy. He smiled at Duncan as they walked into the building.

"It's a bribe," Nate said. "So, she won't fight me too hard on where she's staying tonight."

"I thought as much," Duncan said, opening the door.

Nate paused inside the door, letting the cool air flow over him. "Some days I'm not as acclimated as others, I think. It feels hot out there today."

"DJ said it was 120. I think that qualifies as hot."

"That's hot even for here, they did say something about a heat wave."

"Hey," Dizzy said from her office when she heard their voices.

"Hey," he replied, walking in. Manny was still sitting in front of Duncan's computer, and Dizzy was behind her desk, a scrawl of notes beside her. Doodles ran up the margin of the paper—flowers, squiggles, a skull with holes in it, a smiley face and a couple of arrowheads. He shook his head. "Brought you a coffee." He put the cup down on the only un-papered part of the desk.

"Thanks." She picked up the cup and took a sip with a happy sigh. "We've been chasing antiquities."

"Us too." Nate perched on the edge of the desk. "Duncan found something exciting."

"I never thought I'd have a chance to find something from the Death Pit at Ur, you know, especially not in the middle of the Mojave Desert," Duncan said with a grim laugh. He had settled down next to Manny. She was sipping the coffee Duncan had brought for her.

"Death Pit?" Dizzy asked, her eyebrows climbing. "What?"

"Duncan found an old mine crammed full of stuff, gold statues, jewelry, other things," Nate said.

"We need to get them here!" Dizzy looked from one to the other. "Keep them safe!"

"I thought we'd leave it out there and see who came for it."

"But Nate..."

"Don't worry, I won't let anyone steal the stolen goods. I've got two guys out there at Duncan's dig, keeping an eye on everything."

"Okay, fine. Can I go see?"

"Not today, Diz. You need to get some rest, it's been a long day for you, sun's going down, time to eat and rest," Nate said, taking a deep breath. "Diz?"

"Yes?"

"I don't think you should go home tonight, just in case, stay someplace else."

She looked at him, frowning. "You think I'm in danger?"

Nate shrugged. "I'm not sure. Someone took another run at Greg in the hospital, and if it's the same guy, you might still be on his list. I just think it's wiser for you to not be alone."

"You're right, I guess." She looked over at Manny for a minute. The other woman nodded. Nate had the feeling they'd been talking about this before he and Duncan had arrived. "I..." she said.

"I want you to..." he said at the same moment. They both looked away.

"I think Dizzy should stay with you, Nate," Manny said firmly.

"Manny," Dizzy snapped.

"Well, I think you should, I told you that."

"I think it's a good idea, too," Duncan chimed in. Nate smiled his thanks to the archaeologist.

"Fine," Dizzy said, angrily. "You're right, and I can't take a chance with Manny's life. Give me a couple more minutes, then can we go by my house long enough to get a change of clothes?"

"I'd rather you didn't," Nate said. "Don't you keep some here?"

"I do. I didn't think that ploy would work, but it was worth a shot."

Nate laughed. "You can always try. I'll make a call or two until you're ready." He wandered out towards the reception area of the building. There was no one in there, so he didn't feel bad about pulling out his phone. He called Jack Woods first, seeing how Greg was faring after the incident that morning. There had been no change, but at least Greg hadn't gotten worse.

He called the desk sergeant next. Phil O'Brian had been with the department since before Hades Wells had been incorporated. "What can I do for you, Cap?" O'Brian said.

"Keep an eye on Bob Carter if he's around today, will you?"

"Sure, he's been in and out all day, saw that blonde he's with here, too," O'Brian said. Nate could hear the question in the other man's voice.

"Yeah, she's been around."

"That contractor that works for Carter, the one we busted two months ago for possession, Randy Muntz? He was here today, too," O'Brian went on. "And I saw former council member Carey Scott. God, I hate that guy." O'Brian had been one of the officers who had responded to Dizzy's home seven months before, the night Scott had beaten her.

"I do, too. Thanks, Phil," Nate said, breaking the connection. He wandered back towards the offices, stopping in the small museum and walking through the exhibits. He paused by the statue of Hathor. There was a vase of flowers and a small bowl with fruit in it in front of the statue. He smiled fondly. Dizzy left offerings for some of the things there.

"I'm ready," Dizzy said from the door. Nate turned, she had an overnight bag over her shoulder.

"Good." He turned to her.

"Manny and Duncan are going to stay a bit longer, but I have to admit I'm beat."

He watched her as they walked out to the Jeep. She was slower than usual, she seemed unsteady on her feet, and when they walked out the door into the oven blast of early evening, she actually stopped for an instant. He put his arm around her waist. "You okay?"

"Pretty good for nearly being cooked alive yesterday."

"That's not really funny, Diz." He helped her into the car.

"You're right. Sorry, gallows humor seems to have infected me lately."

"I understand," he said, pulling out into traffic. "Did you find anything on your antiquities hunt?"

"A lot, all depressing as hell. That seller, whoever he is, has a lot of stuff out there. Millions of dollars' worth of stuff." She was quiet, her face thoughtful.

"Diz? What's up?"

"Nothing, just a thought, not really sure what it is yet, just there at the edge of my awareness, you know." She let her head drop back on the seat. "Thanks for this."

"That's what cop friends are for," he said with a laugh as he pulled into his driveway. She waited for him to open her door before getting out, accepting his hand to steady her as the heat hit her again. She walked to the front door and waited for him to open it.

"I might have overdone it a bit today," she said, leaning against the doorjamb.

"You think?" He opened the door. She dropped her bag in the entry way and walked through to the living room, flopping down on the couch and kicking off her shoes.

"This is nice," she said quietly.

Nate picked up her bag and carried it to the spare room. By the time he was back in the living room, Dizzy was sound asleep. He smiled affectionately and pulled a light blanket over her.

Nate made himself a small meal, then checked on Dizzy. She was still asleep on the couch, so he wandered back to his bedroom to watch TV. His phone rang about seven. "Mondragon."

"It's Phil," O'Brian said. "Carter was here part of the afternoon, left with Muntz about three. He was back, alone, about five. Three people came to his office, one I recognized from across the river. The woman arrived around 5:30, they left before six. Thought you'd want to know."

"Thanks. And can you make sure there's a cruiser assigned to the Institute tomorrow?"

"Sure thing, Cap. See ya then."

"Yep."

Nate sighed and leaned back in bed. The information was running through his head. He wasn't sure where it all went yet. He picked up the remote and flipped around for a while, then stopped on a "Scooby Doo" marathon. Halfway through the third episode he was asleep.

"NO!" The shout pulled Nate from his sleep. He sat up in bed and had his gun in his hand before he really registered what was going on. "No, please stop." He ran into the living room. Dizzy was still on the couch, alone, lost in a nightmare. "Please," she was sobbing.

"Diz?" he said gently.

"No, please stop, don't, please."

Nate grabbed her and shook her gently. She tried to pull away from him, sobbing, then opened her eyes. She looked terrified for a moment before recognition flared. "Nate?" Tears were running down her face.

"Hey." He sat down on the couch beside her and pulled her against him. "It's okay." She stiffened for a moment, still in the grip of the nightmare, then leaned against him, crying.

"Sorry, Nate," she said, her voice muffled by his chest.

"It's all right, Diz, everyone has nightmares," he said gently. "Do you want to tell me about it?"

"No, not really," she said. "Just sit with me for a minute?"

"Of course." He turned on the TV. She was quiet against him. After a few minutes, he heard her breathing even out and she dropped off to sleep. Nate shifted, trying to get comfortable without waking her, and let himself slide back into sleep as well.

The automatic coffee pot gurgling to life woke Nate. He lay still for a minute, at first not quite sure where he was, then the night before slowly came back. Dizzy was still nestled against him, her hand resting on his chest. Nate dropped a gentle kiss on the top of her head, enjoying the moment, trying to not move and wake her.

Dizzy rubbed her forehead against his shoulder. "Morning," she said, her voice muffled by his shirt.

"Morning, Diz." He tightened the arm around her shoulders. "How are you feeling?"

"Is your arm totally dead?" She chuckled softly. "I'm okay, the headache is almost all the way gone."

"Good."

She lifted her head and smiled at him. "Didn't make it to bed, did I? No wonder my neck is stiff." She sat up and stretched.

"Yep. Coffee?"

"I think I'll shower first, is that okay?" She stood and walked towards the bathroom, stopping by the spare room to get her things.

Nate wandered into the kitchen and poured himself a cup of coffee. A noise outside drew his attention, he lifted a slat on the shade and looked out. He caught the back end of a pickup pulling away from his driveway. He walked out the front door, the cement had already heated up and burned the soles of his feet. Nate walked under the cover of the ramada to his driveway. There were spots of oil on the pavement. He walked to the other side of the driveway, there were several footprints in the dust alongside the garage. Turning, he headed over to his Jeep, there was a dark puddle on the ground under it. Nate opened the hood, the brake fluid reservoir was empty.

"Very subtle," he said to the lizard sunning itself on a rock by the driveway. "Warning? Or did they want to hurt us? Me or Diz?" He looked at the chuckwalla. "You're not a lot of help."

By the time he'd fixed the line and refilled the reservoir, Dizzy had joined him, bringing him a cup of coffee. She handed him tools as he worked, then trailed behind him as he went back into the house.

"I need a shower," he said, heading back to the bathroom. When he finished, he glanced at the clock and called the office. It was early, but as he suspected, Sal answered her phone. "Morning, Sal."

"Morning, Nate. You sound like hell."

"Thanks."

"Phil left you a note, the mayor called, and someone left a message to call back without a name."

"The mayor called? Sal? It's 7:30 a.m."

"He left a message on voicemail."

"Oh, okay. Charlie in?" Nate asked, knowing his boss's preference for early morning office hours, Charlie's theory being if he got in at seven, he could be done by three. He said it was because of the heat, Nate knew it was because Charlie generally had a four o'clock tee-time.

"Yeah, I saw him about ten minutes ago."

"Can you get him on the horn for me?"

"Sure, might take a minute. I'll have him call," Sal said.

"Thanks, can I get the number without the name?" He jotted down the number Sal gave him.

"Nate? Can you drop me by my house long enough to get my car?" Dizzy asked.

"Nate looked at her for a minute. "Why?"

"I have that survey to finish. It has to be done today. Has to. Has has has to."

"You think by repeating it you can convince me?"

"Nate..."

"Let me make a call or two, then we can get going." Nate took a deep breath trying to calm the anger that had suddenly blossomed in his chest. He knew it was fueled by worry, but that didn't make it easier. He dialed the number Sal had given him. "Nate Mondragon," he said when the connection was made.

"I have information about the killing and the attack on the cop. I need protection," the voice on the other end whispered. "The bastard is going to find me and kill me. I took some shit from him, and if he finds out, I'm dead."

"Okay, come in," Nate said.

"I can't, he'll see me, he's there. Meet me Tuesday afternoon at the Big Wheel truck stop, I'll be in the lot, I'll wait for you." He hung up before Nate could get more information. His phone buzzed in his hand. He glanced at the caller ID. "Hi, Charlie. I want to arrest Bob Carter," he said without preamble.

"He's the bloody mayor, Nate," Rogers said.

"I also think he's a murderer and drug dealer, and more than that as well. I need your permission to move against him."

"Why? No hard evidence?"

"Uh, well..."

"Nothing tying him to it?"

"I have a pretty good idea, Charlie," Nate said and outlined the information he had. "I'm sure it's him, it all fits."

"I don't want to okay that without knowing more. Can you try and get more information before we make the move?"

"I do have someone working on getting that for me. I'll see how that goes and call you back," Nate said, aware of the anger in his voice.

"Sorry, Nate, I just can't let you arrest the damn mayor of Hades Wells without more proof."

"Yes, sir," Nate said and flipped the phone closed. It immediately started ringing. "What?"

"Nate?"

"Sorry, Duncan. What's up?"

"I just got a call from Lisa Daniels, her guy went for it. I'm supposed to pick up the map and go out to look at the lay of the land this evening. It's out at the edge of public land out there by the mountains, kind of out where we were yesterday. Thought you might want to come."

"It's Carter," Nate said definitely. "We just need to figure out a way to have him show his hand."

"Yeah, and get Lisa off my ass," Duncan said with a laugh. "She offered a bonus on top of the fifty."

"Lisa is always fun," Nate said.

"Yeah, fun," Duncan said. "That's what it was, a barrel of fun. You heading in?"

"I need coffee first, the stuff from home is just not cutting it. I'm going to drop Diz off at her car, then I'll meet you there. Duncan..." He stopped when Dizzy walked back into the room.

"Yeah?"

"Talk to you in a few. You about ready? I'll drop you off at your car, but I don't want you out surveying alone."

"I have to go out, Nate. This is what I do. You don't see me trying to keep you from going out on calls, even though I know what can happen, and damn it, Nate!" Tears sparkled at the edges of her eyes.

"Diz?" He took a step towards her. She laid a gentle hand on his cheek. The look in her eyes surprised him. "Diz?"

She smiled. "Later, Nate. We'll talk more tonight, okay?"

"Okay. Tonight."

16

It was early, the light had the soft pink glow that comes just after sunrise. Traffic was still light, most of the commuters not up and moving yet, so Duncan was more or less alone on the road as he drove down towards the coffee shop. The habit of getting up early had not been broken yet, the internal alarm still ringing in time for him to get, at least theoretically, out to the dig. As he eased into the lot at the café, he wasn't surprised to see Nate's Jeep already parked in a "no parking" zone.

The police captain was at a table reading the paper. Duncan ordered a coffee for himself and another for Nate and sat down. "You're here early," he said, pushing the cup across to Nate. "Cardiac tonic, mocha, six shots." He grinned.

"Thanks," Nate said, taking a sip. "I need it. I woke up early but had to do some car repairs before we could leave."

"Car repairs?"

"Someone cut my brake line. Teach me to not set the alarm. I'm sitting here ignoring paperwork for a few minutes before I go into the office. I'm hoping I can avoid one of those days for another hour or two."

Duncan laughed at the look on Nate's face. "Yeah, you look like it's going to be a fun day."

"What's on your plate today?" Nate said so casually Duncan looked up at him with a frown.

"Why?"

"No reason." Nate ran a hand through his hair. "Actually, Diz wants to go out and finish this survey, she has to, she says, and what with the heat stroke and all, I tried to talk her out of it this morning, but she said she had to do it."

"You tried to talk her out of it?" Duncan raised an eyebrow.

"Worked well, too," Nate said ruefully.

"I bet. You want me to offer to do it instead?" Duncan shook his head. "No, she won't go for that, but I can offer to go with her? She might let me do that, never met an archaeologist that turned down another set of eyes. It'll give me a chance to ask her more about the job, too."

"Thanks," Nate said, looking relieved. "There was just no way I could be there today, and I just have a bad feeling for some reason. I have someone watching Carter, but I can't shake this feeling. I'd feel better if you were with her."

"No problem. Should I call? Or just drop by?"

"Drop by where?" Dizzy said from behind him.

"The Institute, Diz," Nate said smoothly. "I was just telling Duncan about that survey you need to finish today."

"Oh?" Dizzy said with an edge to her voice. "Why? Think I need a babysitter, Nate?"

"No." Nate looked down at his coffee.

"I don't need someone to watch over me all the damn time, Nate, I've been doing just fine." She stalked over to the counter to order coffee.

"That went well," Nate said. "Better than I expected."

"Yeah, great. Now what?"

"Well, Duncan? Are you going to leave your car here? Or park it down at the Institute?" Dizzy said, walking back to the table.

"I'll park down there." Duncan stood. "See you later," he said to Nate as he watched Dizzy head out to her car.

"Yeah, and Duncan? Thanks." Nate smiled. Duncan nodded at him, picked up his coffee and followed Dizzy out into the lot.

When he pulled up at the Institute, Dizzy had already gone in. Duncan parked next to Manny's car and headed inside. He could hear raised voices as he walked into the quiet building.

"First Nate, now you," Dizzy was saying as Duncan paused outside Manny's office.

"I just think you should wait a day or two before you go out again." Manny was angry, Duncan had never heard quite that edge to her voice.

"I'm fine."

"You almost died!" Manny snapped. Duncan waited for a reply, but nothing happened. He cautiously pushed the door to the office open. Manny was behind her desk, Dizzy standing across from her. They were both tense, their faces set.

"You about ready?" Duncan said, pretending he hadn't been listening.

"Ready?" Manny said, turning to him.

"Yeah, I'm going out with her today," he said.

"I'll get my stuff." Dizzy walked out of the office. "I'll be right back."

"Thank you, Duncan," Manny said softly. She came around the desk and stood in front of him. On sudden impulse, he bent his head, giving her time to pull away if he had misread the look in her eyes. She wrapped her arms around his neck and kissed him, he leaned into the embrace.

"Uh, hello? Should I just close the door?" Dizzy said.

Duncan pulled away from Manny and turned to Dizzy, expecting to have to defend himself. He relaxed when he realized she had a wide, affectionate smile on her face. "Yeah, ready to go." He turned back and gave Manny a quick kiss before following Dizzy out to her car. He sat down and buckled himself in without looking over at Dizzy.

"About damn time," she said with a chuckle. She turned the car on, gunning it, then flipped on the radio. "I thought I was going to have to lock the two of you in a dark room there for a while."

"Um."

"You hurt her, I'll cut out your liver," she said, looking over at him with a smile.

"Nice, you take the pressure right off, don't you?"

"It's what I do best." She laughed. "Thanks for coming along. I was going to call you, actually, then Nate made a big deal about it and…Never mind. I saw something out there about three weeks ago. I didn't think anything of it, but now, what with everything else, it's bothering me."

"What was it?" he said, bracing himself against the door as she turned onto the dirt road out of town. "You drive like a freak."

"Thanks. It was just a glint of something, off at the edge of the transit line, but now I wonder what it was. I just wrote it off as a piece of glass catching the light, there's a lot of that out there, kids out plinking."

"Plinking?"

"Shooting bottles? But anyway, now I wonder if it wasn't something else. It'd be almost directly in a line down from that trail you and Nate were following the other day."

"Whose land is it?" Duncan said.

"It's part of a section still under Public Lands, right there at the edge of your dig and the new developments." She turned the car up a small wash, Duncan eyed the narrowing walls nervously. "The land kind of sits between the Coyote Estates land on one side and Golden Arroyo Homes on the other."

"Carter and Scott."

"Yes, Public Lands wants it checked since it's so close to the habitations at Cholla Canyon Rock Shelter and that factory site you found. They want to add it into the desert preserve. It's fairly hard to get to, and this deep wash runs through the middle of it. Developers don't want it, about the only people other than us who want it are the punks on ATVs, and anything I can do to frustrate them is a day well spent."

"I agree with you there," Duncan said with a sigh. "I remember my second field school, we were out in New Mexico and these off-roaders came through, they completely destroyed what could have been an important site. It was a factory site, flakes and cores around this huge piece of petrified wood. By the time we got there, what the ATVs hadn't ruined, the guys with the rock hammers had. It was awful. The next time those guys showed up, the head of the dig started shooting at them with her BB gun."

Dizzy laughed. "I didn't know you'd worked for Brenda Means. She got arrested last year for doing that, you know. Turned out one of the punks on the three-wheelers was related to a judge or something. She was in jail for a while. Didn't lose her job though, Phil at the university is kind of down on off-road vehicles too, although I understand she's been cautioned about actually shooting at people."

"Probably not a good idea," Duncan said. He saw the end of the wash fast approaching, he braced himself and held his breath as the wall got closer and closer. They were about thirty feet from the end when Dizzy turned the car up into another track and the Rover shot out onto the desert floor and a wide, well-maintained gravel road. "Jesus."

"You shouldn't swear at the driver like that," Dizzy said, grinning at him.

"I wasn't, I was praying that I'd make it out of this ride alive."

"Ha ha, I know how Nate drives, that doesn't seem to bother you," she said, accelerating.

"Nate's not insane," Duncan said as he watched the speedometer climb.

"I'm not sure about that."

"Less insane than you?"

"Well, yeah, probably that." She smiled. "That's the border of Coyote Estates," she said, pointing at some bright yellow pin flags lining the side of the road. "We're on the utility service road for the Estates and Golden Arroyo Homes." She turned off at a wide spot, parked the car and walked around to the back, grabbing a couple of backpacks she handed one to Duncan. "Do you mind carrying some water? After the other day I've decided to go back to a pack with bottles in it." Duncan could see worry in her eyes.

"No problem," Duncan said, taking a pack and putting a couple of bottles of water in it.

Dizzy put a broad-brimmed hat on her head and closed the back of the car. "Let's go," she said. She started walking at the ground-eating pace that amazed Duncan, for all that her legs were so much shorter than his, she set out at a pace that was a challenge to keep up with. Dizzy led the way to the edge of the mountains. Duncan could see pink pin flags fluttering in the morning breeze. She stopped when they reached the first flag. "This is the beginning of the transit line. I surveyed everything to the north, I wanted to run up the south line today."

"Sounds good, surface survey to the base of the mountains?" Duncan said, looking along the line of flags.

"Sure, three meters apart?" Dizzy asked.

Duncan nodded and paced off roughly three meters, then they started walking slowly up the transit line. As always when he did this kind of work, he focused completely on the ground, noting the color and texture of the stones and other objects on the surface, looking for anything unusual.

He bent down when he saw a small flake, the remnant of a tool used centuries before. He glanced around, there were several other pieces, obviously from the same tool. He dropped a flag in the middle of the scatter and moved on. There was a small pebble, a petroglyph pecked into the surface. He dropped another flag by it, hoping if Dizzy cleared the land, she'd let him add that piece to his article.

Duncan glanced over at Dizzy, she sensed his look and waved. He kept walking. They had been surveying up the line for about an hour when Duncan noticed something glinting at the bottom of a large cliff, the first arm of the mountain reaching out into the desert. He walked over towards the cliff, aware that Dizzy had veered off as well. He glanced up at the mountain. It was essentially right around the corner from where he and Nate had found the cache of objects with the bag of drugs.

"This is where I thought I saw something," she said. "By this rock, I kind of walked this way, but there was a lot of glass lying around, so I thought that's what it was." She shrugged. "I didn't really think much of it, and I admit I got distracted when Bob showed up in one if his Coyote Estates trucks. He was in one of his jolly moods." She laughed. "And I got distracted."

"He can be distracting," Duncan agreed. He could see the very edge of the lab trailer sitting at his dig as he walked towards the cliff. Broken glass was scattered thickly around the base of the large rock, and Duncan was about to turn away, agreeing with Dizzy's earlier assessment, when he caught the glint again, to the left of the rock, right against the cliff itself, close to the dark mouth of an old mine. He walked towards it. "Huh," he said, squatting down. "Dizzy?" She was scouting around the large rock.

"Yes?"

"You better come here, I think I might have finally gone completely insane." Not taking his eyes from the glittering golden object.

"Might have? Only just now gone insane?" she said, laughing. "Thought you were there."

"I'm pretty sure I am now."

She walked up beside him and looked where he was pointing. "Holy crap."

"Yeah."

Dizzy pulled the camera out of her survey bag. "We need pictures. Do we leave it?" She handed him the camera, and he began to carefully take pictures from all angles as she flipped open her phone. "Nate?" She paused as he replied. "I'm fine, mom. Look, Duncan found something out here, kind of goes with all the other strange stuff we've found. Should we bring it in?" Pause. "Well, I don't know, do you think leaving a solid gold torc laying in the middle of the desert is a good idea?" Pause. "Torc, Nate. A piece of Celtic jewelry." She paused again, Duncan looked up at her and she rolled her eyes. "Yeah, we'll bring it in. I'll take it to the Institute.

Sure, hang on, don't talk over me, okay?" She handed the phone to Duncan with a sigh.

"Nate?" he said, handing her the camera. She started going through the pictures.

"I want you guys back here, Duncan. The sooner the better."

"What's up?" Duncan said, glancing at Dizzy.

"We just got a call from the cops in Dryland. They found Lisa Daniels, dead, in her car. She was strangled."

"Oh my god," Duncan said. Dizzy looked up at the tone in his voice.

"And I saw Carter talking to Randy Muntz, and then Muntz headed out of town. I think he's coming your way, and I want the two of you out of there. We know what Carter is capable of, he's already killed two people, maybe three people, tortured Greg, and who knows what else. I need to know the both of you are safe before I make my move."

"Okay, we'll start back now," Duncan said. Dizzy was shaking her head.

"Don't let her talk you out of it," Nate said.

"I won't." Duncan flipped the phone closed and handed it back to Dizzy. "Let's head back."

"No."

"Yes."

"No."

"Yes."

"No, just because Nate is in full-blown mother-hen mode doesn't mean we need to cut this short."

"Yes, we have the pictures, we have the torc. Nate is concerned, and he has good reason. Lisa Daniels is dead."

"What?" She stared at him.

"They found her in her car. Nate saw Carter talking to Muntz, then Muntz headed out of town. We need to go now." He picked up the golden object and started walking away, back towards the car.

"Fine." She stalked after him. She didn't say another word as they walked back to the car, and when they arrived, she wrenched open her door and sat, a sulky look on her face, until he got in the car.

"Dizzy," he said. "I know you're pissed, but he's right. If Carter is behind this, we're all alone out here. If we were caught out here it would be seriously bad."

"You're right." She rubbed a hand over her face. "Let's go."

He smiled at her and looked out the windshield towards the mountains. He thought he saw something glint again. Higher up than where they had been, just the briefest flash, like light caught on a piece of moving glass and then it was gone. He wondered briefly if he should mention it. He glanced up at the cliff and realized with a start that it was the trail he and Nate had scouted a few days before. The trail that led to his dig where the body had been found, the trail that led back to the pass where Dizzy had been attacked, the trail the led up from the canyon where they'd found the cache, and the trail that... Could that be it? Could Nate be that wrong? The strip of land Duncan had signed off on was up against Golden Arroyo Homes.

He realized the car was moving, barreling back down the road towards the wash. He was looking out the window, idly watching a small column of dust off by his dig. He let his mind wander over everything that had happened over the last few days and allowed the pieces to slowly drop into place. They thought Frank was at the center of all of this, Frank and Carter. Maybe it was the other, and right there under their noses. The flights, the cars at odd hours. But could it be that obvious?

Duncan was still musing over those thoughts when the car stopped. He glanced up, they were back at the Institute. He stepped out of the car, debating calling Nate or just heading down to the police station. "I'm going to run into town, take those pictures to Nate, what do you think?" he said, trying to sound casual.

"Good idea," she handed the camera to him. "I'm going to go in and make a few calls, see if I can find out where this came from."

"Maybe you should call Nate and let him know we are back so he can send a cruiser out."

"I'll be fine, Duncan. Manny's here and you'll be at the station in ten minutes, tell him then."

He looked at her for a minute. "I'd like to go on record as not liking it, but okay."

Duncan took the camera and dropped into his car, all the pieces still whirling around in his head. He drove through town, not really paying attention to where he was going, so he was surprised when he automatically pulled into the lot next to Nate's Jeep. Duncan wandered in, smiling at Sal as he walked up to her desk.

"You can go in, but I warn you, he's not a happy camper," she said, grimacing.

"I'll brave it, Sal. I'm bigger than he is," Duncan said, tapping on the door.

"What?" Nate growled from the other side.

Sal raised her eyebrows. "See?"

"It's Duncan," he said, his hand resting on the doorknob.

"Come in," Nate said. Duncan walked in, the police captain looked up, relief evident on his face. "You should have called, let me know you were back. I've had a man on Carter's door for twenty minutes."

"Nate," Duncan said, then stopped, wondering if he had it right or not. "I'm not sure Carter's the right guy."

"What? Of course he is, we have almost proof of the drug flights on and off his land out there. We do have bank records, we know Frank had surveyed his land out there."

"What if Frank found something else?" Duncan said, watching his friend's face.

"Like what?"

"We know he was in that canyon, Nate. All these antiquities, the ones you and I found, the gold bead in his stomach, that statue in the pass, and now today a solid gold torc," Duncan paused, realizing he was thinking out loud. "What if Frank found a cache out there? Like the one that those beads undoubtably came from? We know he was on the take, what if it wasn't Carter he crossed?"

"Who, then?" Nate said, frowning at him. "It has to be Carter, it all fits."

"It does, if we are looking at drugs as the primary motive, but what if drugs aren't? All those damn antiquities. That's what it's about. It's been right there under our noses the whole time. You said, when we found the cache, that whoever it was probably was a user. I don't think Carter is. And if I have that right, then it's someone else. Think about it, Nate, someone who has land out there, someone who has turned up more than once in all of this, someone who, according to you, recently started making more money that his business gives evidence of, someone who knows a fair amount about archaeology and the antiquities trade."

Nate looked at him, comprehension slowly dawning in his eyes. "No, it can't be."

"I'll lay you odds that bastard Austin is in on it, too. We do know things have gone missing from his inventory, including the hand axe in Frank's throat."

"No." Nate was shaking his head. "It has to be Carter."

"DAMMIT, Nate!" Duncan said, slamming his hand down on the desk. "Why won't you see it? It's all there, everything. He'd even know how to find out when her next survey of the pass was planned so they could make a run at her. He came to the hospital to find out if he succeeded. Don't let your hatred of the man blind you to what he did and what he's capable of!"

"What? No," Nate said, anger in his eyes. He picked up the phone and dialed. After a minute he hung up and dialed another number, and another. "No one is answering at the Institute."

"Lines could be down, she might have her cell turned off," Duncan said, trying to push down a sudden feeling of unease.

"Yeah, true, but usually if the lines are down, she turns on her phone."

"What about the cops you have stationed down there?"

"They're not there yet, I didn't know when you two would be back."

"Nate..." Duncan closed his eyes.

"Yeah?"

"When we were out there, after we found the torc, I thought I saw something—like sunlight reflecting off binoculars, maybe. And if someone were there, they might have heard Dizzy was taking the torc back to the Institute."

"Nah, you must have imagined it, probably just a piece of glass catching the sun, Muntz wasn't out there yet." Nate looked at him, his eyes haunted. "He wasn't out there yet."

"I'm trying to tell you it's not Carter, it's not Muntz," Duncan said, frustrated. "And when we were heading in, I thought I saw dust, over on the road by my dig. You wouldn't have to go all that far down the road to get a clear cell signal."

"Shit." Nate was up and out the door before Duncan could react. He caught up with Nate right as he got into his car and gunned the engine. The car was moving before Duncan could get his door closed.

"If I'm wrong, where are you going?" Duncan said, looking over at Nate.

"Just making sure you're wrong," Nate said.

"I don't think I am."

"God, I hope you are, and if you're not..."

"What?"

"I hope we're not too late."

17

The building was quiet, the soft hum of the air conditioner filling the entryway as Dizzy made her way back towards her office. She paused, as always, glancing into the room filled with artifacts. As she rounded the corner, she stopped at Manny's office. Her assistant looked up with a relieved smile on her face.

"You're back sooner than I thought," Manny said as Dizzy walked to her desk.

"Yeah, well, we found something, and Nate called and wanted us back in, so here I am. Didn't get the bloody survey done, yet again." She pulled the torc out of her bag. "Did find this, though."

"What was that doing out in the desert?" Manny asked with wide eyes.

"Hordes of raiding Celts? I don't know, but this can be added to the collection of out-of-place antiquities we've found." She stopped, frowning.

"What is it?"

"That pot, the sherds that Duncan and I found, what if that wasn't a natural? What if it was like this?" She drifted off again.

"Earth calling," Manny said.

"What? Oh, sorry." Dizzy grinned. "Just thinking, and you know what a trial that can be at times. I'm going to put this in the safe," she said, picking up the torc and heading back towards her office, still thinking. She set the torc down on her desk and sank into her chair. Frank had been on the take, what if he'd found the bead and swallowed it to hide it? She remembered Frank's frantic call eight months before. In the mix of angry words, he'd demanded she get out of her relationship. He'd said he had something to show her that would change everything. Of course, he'd never made it to the meeting. She knew why now, but what had that meeting been about? And why did he have the damned bead? Was it something he'd stolen and was planning to sell? Or, she stopped, was it something he'd found and... *Oh.My.God.*

Dizzy picked up the phone to call Nate. There was no dial tone. She got up and wandered out of her office to check the wires. Something made her stop. An odd sound, a muffled noise, but something that set her on edge. She wasn't sure why, but it was a sound that made her stop. She moved closer to the wall to peek around the corner to see what was going on. The building was silent except for the hum of the air conditioner. Dizzy held her breath, listening. She edged closer to the corner to get a better look into the hall and the front of the Institute. As she poked her head around the corner, someone grabbed a handful of hair and pulled her out into the hall.

"I was just wondering when you'd show up," she said, trying to sound casual even as her fear made her heart speed up.

"Figured it out, did you?" he sneered.

"Yeah, I'm sure Nate has, too. It's over."

"Not quite yet." He forced her down onto her knees. "Not quite yet." He held her there for a minute, before yanking her to her feet and forcing her towards the office. She'd left the golden torc lying on her desk. He smiled as he picked it up, dropping it in his pocket. "Open the safe."

"No."

He hit her, a hard back-handed blow, she felt her lip split and the coppery taste of blood in her mouth. "Open it."

Dizzy tried to still the shaking of her hands. She fumbled at the combination and opened the small safe. When she swung the door open, he shoved her aside and rummaged through the small compartment, what he wanted wasn't there. He grabbed her. "Where is it?"

"Where is what?"

"You know what I want. Daniels took it and dropped it, and you found it. In the mountains."

"The statue? Nate has it."

"Lying bitch." He shoved her out the door. "First the statue, then you can join Lisa."

"Lisa?" she said.

"Don't know if you heard, she was strangled and sadly died at my hands."

"What?" Dizzy couldn't keep the horror out of her voice.

"And think your perfect policeman could have saved her, but he didn't."

"I'm sure he tried."

"Always defending him, doesn't matter. Bitch is dead. Open the other safe for me."

She managed to pull away and tried to run. He grabbed her shirt collar to stop her. Dizzy turned, and before he could get his other hand up, she clawed at his face, feeling the flesh tear, bloody streaks appeared on his cheek.

"You'll pay for that, you little bitch, and your friend the cop will too." He dragged her towards the stacks, his hand twisting her collar tight, nearly cutting off her air.

18

Traffic was heavy when Nate pulled onto the highway towards the Institute. The construction on the road was slowing it down even further. He tried to maneuver around the slow down, still resisting the urge to turn on the siren. If Duncan was right, Scott was guilty of at least two murders, maybe more. He took a deep breath, calming himself. Panic would lead to mistakes, and he couldn't afford any more.

A man driving a huge SUV cut in front of Nate, honking and flipped him off. It was too much. Nate waited to a count of three for the guy to stick his hand out the window again and then flipped on lights and sirens. The SUV swerved to the right and off the road. Nate looked at Duncan. "It shouldn't make me so happy when I do that."

"It shouldn't make me so happy, either."

There were three cars in the lot when Nate pulled into the Institute. He parked next to Dizzy's and glanced at the black Mercedes—Scott. Duncan was right. He picked up the radio, "This is Captain Mondragon, I'm at the Institute, can you roll someone over here? We'll need rescue as well."

"Manny's not answering her phone," Duncan said, snapping his phone closed.

Nate got out of the car. "You wait."

"No. You don't know what's going on, it might just be the phones like you said."

"And if it's not?"

"Just as far as Manny's office, Nate. Please."

"No further," Nate said as they walked towards the building. He eased the door open and listened. The building was quiet, he slipped in the door, holding it open just enough for Duncan to follow.

All his senses were on alert. They walked silently through the reception area and past the small museum.

Manny's door was open. Nate stepped inside, freezing when he saw a leg sticking out from behind the desk. He ran around, Duncan right behind him. There was blood on her neck from a wound on her head. He felt for her pulse, sighing with relief when he felt it strong under his fingers. She stirred with the contact.

Nate stood and silently gestured for Duncan to stay with her. He watched as his friend sat down beside her and gently took her hand. Duncan looked up at Nate and nodded, then added a silent "Be careful." Nate gave him a tight smile and eased his gun out of its holster and slipped out of the room.

Dizzy's office was empty, papers thrown around, a pot smashed on the floor. The small office safe was open. Nate moved on down the hallway into the stacks. It was silent, the books absorbing the sound. He stopped, listening, hoping to catch a sound, anything to indicate someone's presence in the building. He slipped further into the stacks, stopping briefly every second or two to listen. Finally, he heard an angry voice.

"You're going to open the safe." Scott's voice bounced off the shelves of books.

"No." Dizzy, defiant, terrified. Nate breathed easier, she was alive and spitting venom, or so it sounded.

"You'll do it," Scott said again. There was the sound of flesh hitting flesh, a tiny yelp reached Nate's ears. He resisted the urge to just barge through the stacks and instead edged ever closer.

"Why?" Dizzy again.

"I'll let you live," Scott said.

"Sorry, don't believe you. You killed Frank and Lisa, you can't let me live. And there's really no point if you're going to kill me anyway," Dizzy said. Nate could hear the fear wavering in her voice as she said it.

"There are ways to die, Dym, some fast and some... not." Scott laughed. "And just like poor dead Lisa, your precious cop isn't coming for you." He laughed again.

Nate heard another noise, a terrified squeak. He moved around the edge of the shelves he was behind in time to see Scott shove her against the shelves, his hand on her neck. Scott tensed for an instant, then, before Nate had time to react, he laughed and, raising his hand, struck her. Dizzy crumpled in a heap. "You move and she's dead," Scott said quietly.

Nate stopped. He set the gun on the shelf next to him, holding his hands out. "I know the combination to the safe, let her go and I'll let you in." He stepped closer to Scott and the other man took a step back, away from where Dizzy lay. "Let's go to the safe," Nate said, keeping his voice calm, trying to get Scott away from Dizzy's prone form. Nate walked towards him, trying to keep out of the man's reach, trying to get Scott to stay focused on him. As he got close, Scott reached out and grabbed him, shoving a gun under his chin. Nate was silently counting, backup should be there in another minute or two. He only needed to distract him that long.

Scott pulled him towards the room with the safe in it, shoving Nate inside and pushing the gun in his lower back. "Open it."

Nate started spinning the dial, clearing the lock. "What do you want in here?"

"She has my statue, the bitch took it and I want it back. I have a buyer waiting for it," Scott said, shoving him closer to the safe. "Hurry."

"You made me screw up," Nate said, spinning the dial again. He braced himself for the blow he figured was coming. It still caught him by surprise, making his head slam into the large safe.

"The only reason you're not dead is you can open this," Scott said. "But if you don't want to, I can always go get the bitch and have her do it before I take care of her." He made a move to step away.

"No," Nate said. "I got it.".

"I thought so."

Nate pulled away as far from Scott as he could and spun quickly through the combination and turned the lever to open the door. As he swung it open, Scott slammed the gun into the back of his head. Nate fell against the door, forcing it the rest of the way open.

Scott turned the gun on Nate. "You all fall over backwards for that bitch, I don't know why." Scott started rummaging through the safe. Nate tried to shift, the gun swung over to him. "Frank Daniels was in love with her, you know. He paid for that admission. Bastard was stealing from me and trying to get in her pants."

"Stealing from you?" Nate said.

"Yeah, first he said he'd sign off on that land I was using, then he refused, and tried to up the ante since he claimed he found something out there. Turns out he took some stuff out of the stash.

Night he died, he had a necklace I'd already sold. It was missing a piece or two. Buyer backed out."

"I found a piece or two of that, part of it was in Frank," Nate said, watching the gun, waiting for an opportunity to take Scott down.

"I wondered. I took a lot of satisfaction in killing him. It felt really good. And then went home to Dym. That was the first night I hit her, you know, that felt good."

"I'm going to kill you," Nate said quietly.

"And then you left your buddy the cop out there, stupid. On a night I made a pickup. That was satisfying too."

"You bastard," Nate snapped.

"And you stayed with her, how touching," Scott growled, still digging through the safe. He finally found what he wanted and turned back to Nate. "I planned on killing her, in the hospital, but you were there." He smirked. "Going to kill her today, though. And guess what? You get to watch and then I'll kill you and be out of the country before anyone figures it out. Ah, here it is." He pulled the statue out.

Nate made his move, diving at Scott and knocking him off his feet. He managed to land a solid punch before Scott swung a hand up, striking out at him, using the green stone figurine as a club. It connected with the side of Nate's face, and he fell back. He saw Scott's gun lying to his left where the man had dropped it and dove towards it. Scott scrambled for the gun as Nate got his hand around it. Scott stomped on his hand and kicked the gun away. The pistol skittered across the floor, stopping against the leg of a table.

Nate got to his knees and made a dive for gun right as Scott got to it and swung it towards Nate.

"Maybe I'll just kill you now," Scott said, leveling the sights on Nate. Abruptly, Scott's focus shifted, and the gun wavered. "You bitch!" He squeezed the trigger, the explosive sound of the shot filling the room.

Nate jerked instinctively but the shot had not been aimed at him. Another gun went off. Scott collapsed as Nate swung to see Dizzy standing behind him in a shooter's stance, his pistol in her hands. He shoved himself to his feet. "Are you hurt? Diz!" He gently took the gun out of her hands.

"Nate?" She blinked at him in confusion, before crumpling against him.

"Diz!" He lowered her to the floor, frantically looking for any sign of a wound.

"How touching, ever the hero," Scott snarled from behind him.

Nate pushed himself up and started to turn in one movement. Scott fired, but the shot went wild, the man was gushing blood from a wound in his shoulder. Nate was bringing his gun to bear when Scott fired again, this one hit home, Nate felt an explosive pain in his left arm as he squeezed the trigger. Scott jerked as the bullet blasted through his chest, and he fell, his eyes locked with Nate's, as he dropped.

Steps were pounding through the building as Nate knelt beside Dizzy again, and lifted her gently into his arms, still looking for the sign of a wound from that first shot.

"Cap!" a uniformed cop shouted as he and his partner burst into the room. "Are you all right? Cap?"

"Yes, thanks, Joe, we need rescue down here for Dr. Donovan."

"What about you?" the older cop said, squatting down and looking at the bloody wound in Nate's upper arm.

"Guy was a bad shot, just grazed me. He attacked and tried to kill Dr. Donovan. He's the bastard that killed Frank Daniels and carved up Greg."

"He dead?"

"Yeah, probably was, I lost my temper," Nate said. He heard the other cop directing the EMTs back to the room. Duncan followed them in, he gave Nate a hand up after Dizzy was on the stretcher.

"You okay" Duncan asked.

"Maybe," Nate said, glancing at Scott's body, a pool of blood surrounded it. "Manny?"

"On her way to the hospital, you should, too, Nate." Duncan put a hand on Nate's shoulder.

"I'm fine!" Nate snapped, then took a breath as a wave of pain and dizziness washed over him. "Okay, maybe not fine. You're right." He handed Duncan his keys. "I'm not going in an ambulance, though." He glanced over at Joe.

"We got it. Already have the place shut down, and you can't investigate your own shooting. They'll be by the ER for a statement, you know the drill, Cap."

"Thanks, Joe," he said, trailing after Dizzy's stretcher. He watched as they loaded her into the ambulance and pulled away. Nate turned to Duncan, and they walked to his Jeep, Nate sliding awkwardly into the passenger seat. Now that the adrenaline was wearing off, his arm was really starting to ache. He dropped his head back against the seat.

"You kill Scott?" Duncan said as he pulled out of the lot.

"Officially, yes," Nate said wearily.

"But?"

"Pretty sure her shot would have killed him, the way he was bleeding, it was bad. It would have taken longer. If he hadn't taken that shot at me, he would have bled out," Nate said, looking over at his friend. "I have to admit, I am kind of glad he gave me the opportunity to kill him."

"She'll need you, after this."

"Don't know about that, Duncan," he sighed. "I just hope this…"

"What?"

"Doesn't kill her, you know," he said softly, letting his eyes close.

Nate noticed the hospital lot was crowded and busy as Duncan pulled up to the ER. He was shifting in his uncomfortably as his arm started to throb. He laughed when Duncan eased the car into a no parking zone and turned the engine off.

"You're learning."

"Thanks! Let's get you looked at," he said as they got out of the car.

"I need to check on Diz."

Duncan grabbed his uninjured arm, steering him through the doors, to the triage desk. "No, you are going to get your arm looked at *first*."

"I need to…"

"Captain Mondragon! We have a room ready for you," the nurse said, stepping around the reception desk and leading them back to an exam room.

"I need to check on Dr. Donovan." Nate tried to break away.

"The doctor is with her now, you might as well let us take care of you until you can see her," the nurse said reasonably.

"Okay, fine."

Duncan sat in the chair, and they waited for the doctor. Surprisingly, they didn't have a long wait. In less than two hours Nate was cleaned up, bandaged and given a sling. The doctor told them he'd been lucky and escaped a broken bone, but it would be "uncomfortable" and he should use the sling to let the arm recover. The nurse brought written instructions and a prescription and then led the way to Dizzy's room. Nate hesitated outside the door.

"I'm going to check on Manny, and fill your prescription," Duncan said, taking the papers from Nate's hands and walking away.

Nate pushed the door open. Dizzy was in the bed with her back to the door. "Diz?"

"Are you okay?" she said without turning to him.

"Yeah, just a flesh wound, and my head's too hard to be hurt, you know," he said gently, walking to the bed.

"Yeah." She turned to him, her face bleak, tear tracks running over a huge bruise marring her face. "Is he dead?"

"Yes," he said as gently as possible.

"Oh." Tears started running out of her eyes again.

"Diz, you saved my life."

"Did I?" she said, looking at him. "I heard you talking to him, and I saw your gun on the shelf. I'm not sure what I was even thinking except it sounded bad. Then he took the shot at me."

Nate put a hand on her shoulder, she pulled away, curling in on herself. "It's over. Thankfully you have a security camera in there. No one will question what happened and the killing shot was mine, Diz. My gun, after all. It's over."

She was still lost, somewhere he couldn't reach her. "I think he wanted going to rape me, Nate, like that night." She started crying, sobbing into her hands.

"He..." Nate swallowed down the bile in his throat. "He *what*? God, Diz, why didn't you tell me?"

"How could I, Nate?" She reached her hand out to him. He took it gently in his own. "I killed him."

"You don't know that, Diz. I fired the last shot."

She snorted. "You know I killed him, Nate."

"Diz..."

"I think I need some time."

"I understand." He took a shaky breath, feeling tears burn in his eyes. "You have my number, when you're ready."

"I do."

He leaned forward and dropped a kiss on her forehead. She squeezed his hand and he turned and walked out the door, down the hall where he could hear Duncan and Manny's voices in quiet conversation.

19

The sun was bright, the heat rising in shimmering waves over the town. The tourists were safely off the roads, workers cool in their office buildings. Hades Wells was quiet, caught in the afternoon heat. Nate drove through town a little faster than he should, a nagging voice kept repeating the speed limit, but he was ignoring it. He was running later than he'd planned. Nate had stopped by to see Greg, who was doing well in rehab, and was hoping to be released in the next week or so.

It was the grand reopening of the Institute, and as the deputy chief of police he was expected to attend. He was both happy and reluctant to go. It was good to see the Institute reopening, but he was nervous about seeing Dizzy. He'd given her the space she asked for, even though it had been a struggle. He was still surprised by the rage her quiet admission in the hospital had created. Once the initial shock had worn off, the rage had started. There was an enormous sense of loss since that day—Dizzy Donovan was a larger part of his life than he had realized or wanted to admit.

He pulled up in front of the Institute, parking next to Duncan's car. Nate grabbed his suit jacket off the seat and stepped out of the car, shrugging the jacket over his shoulders. He'd been freed from the sling two days ago and was enjoying the mobility.

"Nice suit," Duncan said, walking out the door.

"You too," Nate grinned.

"Have to look good since I'm showing off the new office. Besides, Manny would have killed me if I wore shorts and a t-shirt. Not dignified, apparently."

"Yeah, I figured if I showed up casual, Diz would kill me, too. Let's go in before I ruin the damn thing, everyone seems to expect me in the suit all the time."

"How goes it all?" Duncan asked, trying to sound casual. Nate looked over at him and laughed.

"They found another cache out there, where you and Diz found that torc," Nate said. Sometimes it seemed like every law enforcement agency in the world had descended as soon as Dizzy had identified where the torc had come from. Since then, Nate fielded calls on a daily basis from museums and antiquities authorities from around the world. They all wanted to get their hands on the myriad objects found in the desert. The day after the shooting, Nate and Duncan had located another large cache, just at the edge of Duncan's dig, including several pieces stolen from the museum in Dryland. In the days following, they had located three more, full of priceless objects, some stolen from museums, some stolen from burials or other sites.

When Nate had sent someone to the meet at the Big Wheel, they were all surprised when Jacob Austin showed up, demanding protection for all the information he had on Scott. They arrested him on the spot, the trunk of his car contained enough choice antiquities from the museum to put him away for quite a while.

The only thing that got under Nate's skin was that Carter had walked. While he could prove to himself the ongoing drug flights on Carter's land, there was no way to prove it to anyone else unless they caught them red-handed, and the flights had stopped for the time being. Carter had bank records showing deposits from legitimate companies, but Nate still knew they were from the drug money. He could feel it in his bones. He sighed as they stepped into the air-conditioned building.

The building was noisy, the usually quiet reception area full of people. The front desk was covered with trays of finger food and champagne. The small museum was crowded, people wandering through the display. Nate knew most had never been in the building before, showing up now for free food and booze—and the chance to get a look at the "scene of the crime."

He followed Duncan through the building, stopping as his friend ushered him into his office. Duncan handed him a champagne flute. "Don't worry, it's sparkling cider, but we have to break in the office, right?"

"Glad you decided to accept her offer," Nate said, smiling. He had to admit he'd been relieved when he heard that Duncan had accepted the position of resident archaeologist Dizzy had offered him at the Institute.

"Well, the department chair was pissed the dig is closed for the season, somehow he thinks it's my fault." Duncan laughed. "Oh, and this salary is way more than what I was making as a prof. Even though I think my title is actually something like 'Official Director of Everything He Ends Up Doing.' That's what Dizzy implied at least"

"Has nothing to do with Manny, of course."

"Nothing at all, nope." He smiled.

"I didn't think so," Nate said, draining his glass. "Well, Mr. Resident Archaeologist, shall we mingle?"

They wandered out into the museum. Nate moved from one group to another, answering shallow questions. Duncan saved him more than once from sweet older women who latched themselves onto his arm like pit bulls. He would catch a glimpse of Dizzy every now and then, flitting at the edge of the group. She was her usual acerbic self, and he noticed more than one person walk away, either with a grin or a frown. Nate watched Duncan and Manny slip out of the room, returning several minutes later, broad smiles on their faces. The afternoon wound into early evening, until finally the museum was empty except for the four of them. Nate, Duncan and Manny were clearing the glasses off display cases. Dizzy had disappeared to take a call from a European museum.

"Nate?"

He put the tray of glasses and paper plates down and turned to her, Duncan and Manny were nowhere to be seen. "Hey," he said, unsure of what else to say. His voice sounded strained to his ears.

"I, uh...sorry," she turned to leave.

"Diz, please," he said, taking a step towards her.

"What?"

"We need to talk."

"About what?" she said, a snap in her voice.

"Uh." He was suddenly unsure. All the practiced speeches, all the things he wanted to say stopping somewhere between his brain and his mouth.

"Yes?"

"Diz, I..."

"I know, Nate."

"Not really. Not this time. I don't think you do know."

"Don't know what?"

"You saved my life." He raised his eyebrows. "You know what that means."

"What does it mean?"

"I owe you my life, you know, that old life-debt thing?"

She smiled. "You saved me first. So, I guess we're even."

"I like that, Diz."

"I killed him, Nate. I have blood on my hands."

"I have some on mine too," he said, still closer, he could almost touch her.

"And he killed poor Frank, and Lisa. And..."

He took the last step, hoping it wasn't a mistake. "Yeah," he said gently. "You should have told me."

"I didn't want you to think..."

"What?"

"Less of me, you know, for letting that happen to me. He said...and then I heard him telling you, and I was afraid, and I thought you would..." She looked down. "I thought you would hate me, Nate."

"Oh, Diz, no, never." He pulled her into his arms and gently stroked her hair. "It's going to be okay, Diz. We'll get through this."

"Maybe," she said softly.

"No maybes, Diz, we'll get through. I promise," he said. "And we'll be stronger because of it."

She started laughing and leaned back to look at him. "Leave it to you to come up with the sappy Nietzsche-esque thought."

"I've been saving that one. There're just not enough chances to use Nietzsche, you know." He laughed softly, then sobered. "I mean it, though, Diz."

"I know you do," she said, allowing him to pull her against him again. "And I'll do my best, I promise."

"Can't ask for more than that," he said gently.

"Hey," Duncan said, coming into the room with Manny. Nate looked up, over Dizzy's head, at his friend. Duncan nodded towards Dizzy's office. "All set," he mouthed silently.

"What?" she said, looking at Nate before turning to Duncan.

"Ready for dinner? Real food? Manny just called Ted, there's a table waiting at Mango Tree for us."

"Sounds good," Dizzy said, linking arms with Manny and walking out of the room. "Don't be long or I'll find the horn, you know."

"I know, Diz," Nate said with a laugh.

"Everything okay" Duncan said quietly.

"I think it might be," Nate said as they followed the women out of the building into the soft warm desert night. "Just as long as we can avoid one of those days for a month or two. Summer will be over soon, and once it cools off, it's easier to survive in Hell."

Nate laughed softly and slid into the driver's seat beside Dizzy. She smiled at him as he turned on the car and pulled out onto the highway into town.

20

The sun was just cresting the mountains as Dizzy pulled into the parking lot at the Institute. The lot was still empty. Duncan was due at any time, they had a survey scheduled and they both wanted to get out as early as possible. The heatwave that had started the day before was in full swing. It was their first official day open, and they wanted to get right back into things.

She walked in, everything was quiet. The flowers from the Grand Re-Opening were still on the tables, their scent filling the room. She took a moment to wander through the building. The chaos wrought by the investigation was completely gone. They'd decided to shift the stacks around, the safe had been moved and the area where the shooting had happened was walled off. It wasn't a loss of that much space, and she'd decided to spend some of their budget and get a new shelving system for the books and other printed materials that held more items but, in the end, took less space. They were also more efficient as shelving went, and it gave them a chance to revamp the catalog as well.

Dizzy sighed, she'd been trying too hard to keep herself occupied. Work had been busy, more than busy, as she dealt with the investigation into artifacts Duncan and Nate had found. The calls seemed non-stop some days. Maybe they were. She did know that between the calls, the work on the Institute and her usual pile of work most days she was so tired at the end of the day she'd just go home and fall into exhausted slumber.

She missed her life. She'd realized that last night as they all sat around the table at Mango Tree. Since the shooting, she'd stopped going by to get coffee in the morning, stopped going to the Inn, pretty much stopped everything but work. It felt empty. Dizzy knew it was partially because she hadn't wanted to risk running into Nate and seeing something—Hate? Disappointment? Loathing? in his eyes. She thought he'd been avoiding her, and she didn't have the heart to ask when he did call. Somehow, she couldn't find it in herself to say she missed things.

They'd talked some last night. Maybe, just maybe, she could get her life back.

Finally, she turned to her office. Duncan was picking up coffee, he'd probably gossip with Nate for a minute or two, maybe she could get a little work on the grant application done before he arrived. She opened the door and stopped.

"My sheep!" she whispered in the quiet room, feeling tears prick at the corner of her eyes.

Set carefully on the small worktable was the panel that had been stolen from the cave at Windy Pass. The little family of bighorn sheep she loved. On top of it was a handwritten note:

I can't put them back where they were taken from, but I can make sure they are in your care —— Nate

Author's Note

    I'd like to thank everyone who has helped with this book along the way. Readers, editors and general get back to work, Muffy-ers. This story has been waiting for a long time. It first saw the light of day many years ago, and has changed and grown. I am hoping this is the first in a series.

    I hope my deep love of the desert shines here. This is something of a love letter to an empty, stark, harsh land I love dearly.

Made in the USA
Columbia, SC
08 November 2024